R.L. STINE'S

GHOSTS OF
FEAR STREET ®

NIGHT
OF THE
WERECAT

R.L. STINE'S
GHOSTS OF
FEAR STREET ®

NIGHT
OF THE
WERECAT

ALADDIN
NEW YORK LONDON TORONTO SYDNEY

ALADDIN
An imprint of Simon & Schuster Children's Publishing Division
1230 Avenue of the Americas, New York, NY 10020
This Aladdin paperback edition May 2011
Copyright © 1996 by Parachute Press, Inc.
Night of the Werecat written by Katherine Lance
All rights reserved, including the right of
reproduction in whole or in part in any form.
ALADDIN is a trademark of Simon & Schuster, Inc.,
and related logo is a registered trademark of Simon & Schuster, Inc.
FEAR STREET is a registered trademark of Parachute Press, Inc.
For information about special discounts for bulk purchases, please
contact Simon & Schuster Special Sales at 1-866-506-1949
or business@simonandschuster.com.
The Simon & Schuster Speakers Bureau can bring authors to your live event.
For more information or to book an event contact the Simon & Schuster Speakers Bureau
at 1-866-248-3049 or visit our website at www.simonspeakers.com.
Manufactured in the United States of America 0411 OFF
2 4 6 8 10 9 7 5 3 1
Library of Congress Control Number 2011920436
ISBN 978-1-4424-2698-6

R.L. STINE'S

GHOSTS OF

FEAR STREET ®

NIGHT
OF THE
WERECAT

You can do this, Wendy. Concentrate.

Wendy Chapman focused all her attention on the four-inch-wide beam. Gymnastics was her favorite after-school club. But the balance beam terrified her.

"Looking good," her best friend, Tina Barnes, called.

I won't fall this time. I won't! The floor was so far below. Wendy took a deep breath. She fought back her terrible fear of heights. It didn't help that she had never been very surefooted.

Halfway across, she steadied her outstretched arms. But she could feel her balance beginning to waver.

"Pssssssst!" Wendy glanced toward the sound coming from the bleachers. Nancy Morrow's smirking face caught her eye. Nancy hissed again, then windmilled her arms. She was imitating someone falling!

Wendy forced her eyes back to the beam. Forget Nancy! she scolded herself. Concentrate on the balance beam.

But it was too late. That glance away made her dizzy. Wendy teetered, then fell off the beam. Ms. Mason, her gymnastics coach, stopped Wendy from crashing onto the mat. But she landed awkwardly and stumbled forward.

"What's the matter, Wendy?" Nancy taunted. "I thought cats always landed on their feet." She began laughing, and some of Nancy's snobby friends joined in.

Wendy's face burned with embarrassment. Nancy was always teasing her!

"That's enough, Nancy," Ms. Mason said. She patted Wendy's shoulder. "It was a good try, Wendy. You're improving."

"Thanks," Wendy said faintly. She faked a smile. But inside she felt awful. On Saturday the top three girls in the club would be chosen to represent Shadyside Middle School at the all-city meet. I'll never make the team now, Wendy thought sadly.

On the way to the locker room, Nancy bumped into Wendy. "Maybe your little cat friends can give you lessons, Wendy," she said with a sneer. "Cats have good balance, don't they?" Nancy smoothed back her perfectly combed, shiny black hair.

Self-consciously Wendy pushed her own thin blond

hair out of her face. "Leave me alone!" Wendy snapped.

"Gee, I thought it was a great idea," Nancy went on. Her voice sounded sweet, but Wendy knew better. "I thought you'd *love* to be more like a precious kitty cat."

"Why can't Nancy leave me alone?" Wendy complained as she and Tina left school after Gymnastics Club.

Tina shrugged. "She's just jealous because you skipped a grade." Wendy had skipped fifth grade. Most of the other kids in sixth grade were twelve, but she was barely eleven. But that didn't bother Wendy. Her mother said Wendy was advanced for her age. "Don't worry," Tina continued, tightening her long, brown ponytail, "Nancy will find someone else to pick on sooner or later."

"Well, I wish she'd do it soon!" Tina and Wendy looked both ways, then crossed over to the bus stop. "And why does she hate cats so much, anyway?" Wendy couldn't imagine how anyone could dislike the beautiful animals.

"Didn't you know?" Tina asked. "She's really allergic to them. Her brother told me if she even gets near a cat, she breaks out and starts sneezing."

"I wish I had a cat to stick right under her nose right now!" Wendy declared.

Tina giggled. Her big, brown eyes twinkled. "Maybe you can get one at the cat show."

The Shadyside cat show opened that afternoon.

3

Wendy and Tina had been looking forward to it for weeks.

"If only." Wendy sighed. She loved cats. But her parents wouldn't let her have one.

A red city bus pulled up to the stop. "Cat show, here we come!" Wendy cheered. She and Tina slapped each other high fives, then boarded the bus.

The cat show took place in an empty store across from the Division Street Mall. As the girls stepped off the bus, Wendy glanced up. She spotted a large banner stretched across the front of the building.

"There it is! The Shadyside Cat Circle Breeders' Show," she read aloud. She grabbed Tina's hand and they ran to the entrance. The mews and meowing from inside seemed to be calling Wendy's name. She was in such a hurry that she almost forgot to wait for her change when she paid the fifty cents admission!

The big room was filled with long tables. Cages containing cats and kittens stood on each table. Their owners sat behind them.

Wendy's eyes widened. "I've never seen so many cats!" she exclaimed. "I could spend the whole week here!"

Tina chuckled. "I like cats, too," she commented. "But nobody is as cat-crazy as you."

"I know," Wendy agreed. "I love them. Do you think my parents would notice if I stayed here forever?"

They wandered up and down the aisles. Wendy didn't know where to look first. All those beautiful cats! Each sweeter than the last.

Wendy stopped at a blue cage containing a long-haired brown and white striped cat. It was nearly as big as a cocker spaniel.

"Cyril is a Maine coon cat," the owner told her. "Would you like to pet him?"

"Oh, could I?" Wendy reached into the cage and stroked the silky fur. Her heart melted when the cat purred and licked her hand.

"I wish my parents would let me have a cat," she said for the millionth time. "When I grow up, I'm going to have a huge house filled with cats and kittens!"

"Look at this, Wendy," Tina called. Wendy said good-bye to Cyril and joined her friend at a side door. It led into a much smaller room. The room was empty except for a large booth. Blue curtains covered with cat stickers hung from hooks shaped like little cat heads. The curtains were pulled shut.

Wendy stepped into the room. "Mrs. Bast's Cat Curios," she read from the sign over the booth. The letters were made up of colorful paw prints.

Tina stopped beside her. "It looks closed," she said.

"Let's check it out, anyway," Wendy suggested. "I think Mrs. Bast has my kind of shop."

"Just remember what your mom said about spending more money on cat things," Tina warned.

"Don't worry, I'm not going to buy anything," Wendy reassured her. "Unless I really, really have to have it," she added with a giggle.

Wendy approached the booth. "Hello?" she called. "Mrs. Bast?"

No response.

"Maybe I should meow," Wendy joked. "Maybe Mrs. Bast only serves cat customers."

"There's no one here," Tina said. "Come on, Wendy, let's go back to—"

"Please, Tina, I just want to peek inside. I have to find out what's here." Wendy reached out to part the curtains. Instantly a hand shot out from inside and grabbed her wrist.

Startled, Wendy tried to free herself. But she couldn't. The grip was too strong.

Wendy's heart nearly stopped. She felt herself falling through the thick blue curtains!

2

"**H**elp!" Wendy screamed. "Tina!" The curtains smacked Wendy in the face as she fell into the booth. She struggled against the strong hands that gripped her. "Help!"

The hands let go. Wendy stumbled backward a few steps.

"Welcome!" a voice croaked.

Wendy blinked. Across from her stood an old woman, wearing a long red dress. A beautiful hand-painted cat covered the front of it. The woman's frizzy white hair surrounded her face like a cloud.

"I'm Mrs. Bast," the old woman announced. Her whole face crinkled up into a zillion wrinkles when she smiled at Wendy.

7

"Wendy!" Tina cried, rushing through the curtains. "Are you all right?"

"I'm f-fine," Wendy stammered. She rubbed her wrists. For an old woman, Mrs. Bast had some grip.

"You're my first customers," Mrs. Bast told them. She flung apart the curtains. "I was just getting ready to open the booth when you showed up." She grinned at the girls. "I could hear you through the curtains. I didn't want you to get away. I knew you would appreciate fine cat curios."

A mewing sound caught Wendy's attention. On the counter behind Mrs. Bast stood a long-haired white Persian cat. "Ohh," Wendy breathed. "Is that your cat?"

Mrs. Bast gave the cat a pat on the head. "This is Samantha," she said. "She's my assistant. She chooses what I should sell." Mrs. Bast began bustling around the booth. "Samantha has very good taste."

Wendy reached out and gently touched the Persian's back. Its long white fur was as soft as a silk scarf.

"She likes you," Mrs. Bast commented.

"All cats like Wendy," Tina said.

"And I like all cats," Wendy added. She scratched Samantha under the chin. The white cat began to purr. It was Wendy's favorite sound.

Mrs. Bast rubbed her hands together. "What are you looking for today?" she asked. "Jewelry? Photos? T-shirts? Knickknacks? I've got them all!"

Wendy turned her attention from Samantha to the shelves and displays in the booth. There were trays of cat pins, earrings, bracelets, and necklaces. T-shirts hung from a rack. A clothesline across the top of the booth held posters of lions, tigers, cheetahs, and panthers.

"This is pretty," Tina remarked. She held up a purple bracelet made of cat-shaped beads.

Wendy poked through a tray on the counter labeled "All items $5." A shiny object caught her eye. "Tina, look!" she exclaimed. She held up a silver chain. A delicate metal charm of a black cat dangled in front of her eyes. In the center of the cat's forehead was a spidery white star.

Tina turned to see the necklace. "It's pretty," Tina agreed. "But what's that weird white spot on its face?"

"That's what I like best about it," Wendy said. She ran her finger lightly over the white mark. It was so unusual. And the cat looked so real! "I'm going to take this," Wendy told Mrs. Bast. She held out the charm.

The old woman glanced at the trinket and gave a startled gasp. Then she scowled. "That charm isn't for sale," she snapped. In a quick move Mrs. Bast snatched the necklace from Wendy's hand.

Wendy was shocked. "But why not?" she blurted. "It was in the tray with all the other cat charms."

"It's not for sale," Mrs. Bast repeated. "And it's not a cat charm. It's a *were*cat charm. That white star on its face is the mark of the werecat."

Werecat? Wendy glanced at Tina. Tina raised her eyebrows.

"What's a werecat?" Tina asked.

"Have you heard of werewolves?" Mrs. Bast demanded.

"Everyone's heard of werewolves," Wendy replied. "They're people who supposedly turn into wolves when the moon is full."

"Werecats are the same," Mrs. Bast said. "Only they turn into cats. Very large, very wild cats. And they do it every night, whether the moon is full or not."

Tina snorted. "But werewolves aren't real," she protested.

"I don't know about werewolves," the old woman said. "But werecats are very real indeed." She poked her head out of the booth and glanced around. Seeming satisfied no one was listening, Mrs. Bast continued. "I've seen them myself," she whispered. "Right here in Shadyside. They prowl the Fear Street Woods."

Wendy looked at Tina and they both smiled. They loved stories about Fear Street.

Everyone told stories about the creepy things that happened on Fear Street. But Wendy had been in the Fear Street Woods lots of times. And except for twisting her ankle once when she tripped, nothing terrifying ever happened to her! Still, she and Tina loved to hear all the Fear Street rumors.

"After midnight," Mrs. Bast continued in her croaking voice, "that's when the werecats roam."

"Like alley cats?" Wendy asked.

Mrs. Bast shook her head. "Not at all. You would

never mistake a werecat for an ordinary alley cat. A werecat is more daring. All its senses are sharper. It can see, smell, and hunt better. Even its balance is better than a regular cat's. Werecats are beautiful, fierce creatures."

"My cat, Shalimar, is fierce when I don't feed him." Tina giggled. "Maybe he's really a werecat!"

"Maybe we should bring Shalimar over to the Fear Street Woods!" Wendy joked.

"Hah!" Mrs. Bast's barking laugh made Wendy jump. "A werecat would attack your Shalimar if he got in its way. Werecats and regular cats are mortal enemies."

"Shal can take care of himself," Tina insisted.

"He wouldn't stand a chance with a werecat," Mrs. Bast replied. "They run on pure instinct, and they are very powerful. And just like an ordinary cat, werecats are territorial. A werecat will defend its home to the death."

"Why do they only appear after midnight?" Wendy asked. She didn't believe a word Mrs. Bast said, but she liked any story about cats. Especially one that included Fear Street.

"All cats are nocturnal," Mrs. Bast explained. Her voice dropped to a whisper. "But late night is the time of the werecat. And as the moon grows fuller, the werecat grows wilder. There's no way to predict what it will do."

"But if they turn back into people by day, don't they think like humans?" Wendy demanded.

"During the month there is a bit of the human left

in a werecat," Mrs. Bast agreed. "But when the moon is full, the human no longer has any control over the animal. And once the werecat experiences its first full moon, the transformation is complete."

"What do you mean?" Wendy asked.

"After that first full moon the werecat inside begins to do things—even in human form. Even during the day. The human and the cat blend together."

Mrs. Bast fell silent. Wendy thought the story was over. She glanced at Tina, and Tina rolled her eyes. She obviously thought Mrs. Bast was nuts.

But now Wendy wanted the cat charm even more. "What a cool story!" she told Mrs. Bast. "Please, I have to buy the charm now. It will be my favorite cat jewelry!" She held out a five-dollar bill.

"No!" Mrs. Bast snapped. "I cannot allow you to have it. It wouldn't be right!"

Wendy stared at the old woman. What was Mrs. Bast's problem?

"Come on, Wendy," Tina murmured. She tugged Wendy's sleeve. "Let's go look at some more cats."

But Wendy wouldn't give up. She wanted the charm!

"Please, Mrs. Bast—" she began again. But before she could say anything else, the white cat leaped off the counter and slipped under the curtain.

The old woman gasped. "Samantha! Come back here!" She dropped the werecat charm and hurried after the cat. Tina followed her out of the booth.

Wendy's heart stopped. The beautiful charm lay on the table. Right in front of her hand.

I found it in the five-dollar tray, Wendy told herself. There was no reason why she shouldn't have it. Besides, it wasn't as if she were *stealing*. She would pay for it.

Wendy could hear Mrs. Bast and Tina moving behind the booth. "Samantha," Mrs. Bast crooned. "Here, sweetie."

Her hand shaking, Wendy slowly placed the five-dollar bill on the tray. Then she grabbed the necklace and looped it around her neck. She quickly fastened it and slipped it inside her T-shirt.

She did it! She couldn't believe she actually did it! Her heart pounded in her chest. She felt a strange tingling sensation where the charm touched her skin.

"Tina!" Wendy called. "Let's go!" She wanted to get out of the booth before Mrs. Bast noticed the charm was gone. But I didn't steal it, she told herself again.

Tina popped her head into the booth.

"Let's get back to the show," Wendy said.

Tina looked puzzled. "But—"

Wendy quickly interrupted her. "Isn't it time to meet your mom?"

Tina glanced at her watch. "Ooops," she said. "You're right."

"Got to go, Mrs. Bast!" Wendy called over her shoulder. She and Tina hurried back to the main hall.

Wendy stepped into the huge room, then stopped in surprise. The moment she entered the room, she heard a horrifying sound. She and Tina stood still.

A terrible wailing filled the air. Wendy shuddered. Her entire body tensed.

The sound grew louder and weirder.

A chill ran up Wendy's spine, and she clapped her hands over her ears. She couldn't stand it.

It was the most terrifying sound she had ever heard.

3

The screeching sound grew louder. Louder. Wendy searched the room, frantically trying to find out where the sound came from. Then her mouth dropped open in surprise.

The horrible wailing came from the caged cats!

"What's wrong with them?" Wendy cried.

"I don't know!" Tina shouted over the noise. "But it's awful! Let's get out of here."

They ran through the exhibits, their hands covering their ears. But they could still hear the terrible sound. They raced by table after table of screeching cats. As Wendy passed Cyril's cage, a furry paw reached out and clawed her.

The moment they stepped through the exit, Wendy

15

heard something even stranger. Silence. The yowling had stopped.

Tina and Wendy slowly lowered their hands. They stared at each other for a moment.

"That was totally weird," Tina finally said.

"Totally," Wendy agreed. What could have made the cats act like that? she wondered.

"How was the cat show, sweetie?" Wendy's mother asked as Wendy entered the kitchen.

"It was great." Wendy let out a huge sigh. She flopped into a chair at the table. "I saw about a hundred cats that I wanted to bring home."

"You always want to bring cats home," her mother teased with a warm smile. As she bent over the stove, her pale blond hair fell across her face.

"*Why* can't we have a cat?" Wendy began the familiar argument. "Why don't you and Dad like them?"

"It's not that we don't like them, Wendy," her mother replied. "It's that we don't want them in the house. There's a difference."

"What if we kept it outside?" Wendy continued.

"Cats have a way of getting in," Wendy's mother said firmly.

"Yeah," Wendy's older brother Brad agreed, strolling into the kitchen. Brad was a junior in high school. His hair was black, and lately he wore it in a ponytail. "Cats are sneaky," Brad went on. "I'd rather have an armadillo." He pulled a half gallon of milk from the refrigerator and drank from the carton.

"Brad!" Wendy's mother scolded.

Wendy watched her brother sadly. Wendy remembered that Brad used to love cats as much as she did. But now he didn't want one, either. Wendy was outnumbered. This was a battle she would never win.

Standing at her mirror that night, Wendy pulled the cat necklace out from under her shirt. She stroked the cool metal. I wish it were real, Wendy thought. I wish I really had a cat.

She changed into her nightgown and crawled into bed. She patted the charm again. She thought of all the beautiful cats she had seen that day. Cats that would never be hers.

At least I can dream about them, she thought as she fell asleep.

Later that night Wendy woke up suddenly. A bright light shone through the window. She glanced at her bedside clock and noticed that it was one minute to midnight.

What was that light? Wendy got up and peered through the window. She could see the moon rising through the old oak tree in the side yard.

Weird, she thought. The moonlight never woke her up before. Was it always that bright? She started to climb back into bed when she felt a warm spot on her chest. She glanced down. The cat charm seemed to be glowing with a greenish inner light.

She held it between her fingers, trying to get a better look at the glowing light. Her fingertips tingled where she touched the charm.

What is going on? Wendy wondered.

The tingling spread. From her fingers into her hands and up her arms. A strange itchy feeling moved down her back and chest, covering her whole body. She felt warm all over.

I must be getting sick, she told herself. *That's it. I'm sick.*

But this didn't feel like any flu or cold she had ever had before. Besides, Wendy didn't feel sick, exactly. Just . . . peculiar. Then her fingertips began to ache. What would make that happen? she wondered.

All ten of her fingers throbbed now. Her fingernails actually hurt. Puzzled, she held them up to her face.

In the bright moonlight she could see that her fingernails were very long, much longer than she remembered them. How could they have grown so fast?

Wendy's heart began to beat faster. What's happening to me?

She took a closer look at her hands.

Fear rose in her throat. Fear so strong it almost choked her.

Sprouting from the tips of her fingers weren't fingernails.

They were long, sharp, curved claws.

4

"**N**o!" Wendy whispered in horror.

Wendy couldn't tear her eyes away. She could see the claws grow longer. Her fingers started to shrink—becoming shorter and thicker. Her stomach churned as she watched long reddish-blond hair sprout on the backs of her hands.

She tried to move her fingers but couldn't. They had fused together. Her hands looked exactly like paws!

Her whole body itched. She glanced down. Fur was growing on her arms, her legs, her chest. Everywhere!

Her ears tickled. She reached up with her furry paws to touch them. Her ears were changing shape. And somehow they had moved to the top of her head.

What is happening to me? Wendy thought. She

shut her eyes, too terrified to watch the terrible changes taking place.

She felt her face twist as her nose and mouth moved closer together. The inside of her mouth became dry and strange. She touched her teeth with her tongue. Her teeth were now sharp and pointed.

"No!" she cried aloud. But this time the word came out as *Noooooowwwwww!*

Wendy's heart pounded so hard she could hear it. She tried to sit up. Her balance was all wrong, and she fell off the bed. But instead of landing on her back, she landed on her feet—all *four* feet!

Terrified, Wendy jumped up on her dresser and gazed into the mirror.

She couldn't believe it. This must be a dream.

A cat gazed back at her.

A tawny-colored cat with a white star on its forehead.

Wendy turned her head. The cat in the mirror turned, too. When she lifted her hand, it lifted its front paw.

It can't be! Wendy thought. It can't!

But she knew the truth.

The cat in the mirror was Wendy.

Wendy was a cat.

A cat with a white spot on its forehead.

Mrs. Bast's words echoed in her mind. *"The white star is the mark of the werecat."*

I'm a werecat! Wendy realized.

The necklace she wore transformed into a tightly

fitting silver collar with the metal werecat charm embedded in the front.

I'm trapped! Wendy thought. What will I do?

Her heart beat so quickly Wendy thought it might explode. She arched her back, watching the cat in the mirror arch, too. She glanced around, confused and frightened.

And saw the open window.

Suddenly Wendy felt as if invisible hands were pulling her to the window.

Outside. I must go outside.

Wendy bounded across the room and jumped up onto the windowsill. She gazed down at the yard two stories below. She glanced across at the old oak tree. Its largest branch was about three feet from the window.

Without even thinking, she leaped out the window. She landed easily on the branch, her sharp claws grasping the rough bark. She scurried down the tree trunk.

She was out!

Wendy loped across the dewy grass. She could see better than she ever had in daylight. The moon cast sharp shadows in the corners of the yard. She tracked dozens of tiny insects, crawling in the grass or flying through the air.

Her sharp ears picked up sounds all over the neighborhood. She heard dogs growling, babies crying, people snoring. She even heard the rustling of birds in their nests.

Wendy leaped up and over the backyard wall, into the alley. Strange and delicious odors floated all around her. *Mmmmmmm.* A wonderful fish smell came from the next-door neighbor's garbage can. She jumped onto the can and began pawing at the lid.

Before she could pry open the lid, a movement at the end of the alley drew her attention. Wendy sniffed the air until a strong scent filled her nostrils. Her cat-senses told her it was the scent of a mouse.

Forgetting about the fish, she leaped off the garbage can. She streaked to the corner, where the mouse vanished into a thick tangle of grass and weeds. Wendy wasn't bothered by its disappearance. She knew exactly where it was. She could hear its foot-steps. She could hear its faint squeak.

Her mouth began to water.

Wendy hunched down, then sprang. Her paws landed on the mouse's tail. The creature pulled away. It scampered deeper into the grass. Wendy let it go. For the moment. She was still just playing with the little rodent.

Wendy hunched down again. Again, she pounced. And once more the mouse was under her paws. But now Wendy was ready for the game to be over. She extended her claws, ready to bring them down on the mouse.

SKREEEEEEEEEEEEEEEEEEEE!

A terrifying high-pitched wail filled the night air.

Wendy sat up. The terrible noise in her ears was the alarm clock. She punched it off.

22

She blinked a few times. Her mind was still full of her adventures as a cat.

What a cool dream, she thought, stretching. And it seemed so real. She loved cats so much, it was natural she'd dream about being one!

Wendy climbed out of bed and put on her jeans and a blue shirt with an orange cat on the front. She stood at her dresser mirror and admired the werecat charm hanging around her neck. But she couldn't let her parents see that she had bought more cat jewelry. Not yet. She tucked the charm under her shirt.

She stuffed her sandy hair into a yellow scrunchie. Then she kneeled down to pull her shoes out from under the bed.

And stopped in horror.

There, right beside her sneaker, lay a dead mouse.

5

"Yikes!" Wendy yelped. She yanked her hand back. Yuck! She'd almost touched it!

Where did that mouse come from? she wondered. Was the dream real? Did I really turn into a werecat last night?

Wendy giggled. Yeah, right, she teased herself. Now you really *are* being cat-crazy.

She glanced at the mouse and shivered. How was she going to get rid of it? Just the thought of touching the mouse made her feel sick.

Her door banged open.

"Yo, Wendy!" Brad popped his head into her room. "You better move it if you want to ride with me to school."

"Uh, I'm almost ready," she told her brother. "There's just one thing. . . ."

"What?" Brad stepped into the room.

Wendy scrunched up her face and pointed to the dead mouse.

Brad glanced at the animal, then laughed. "How did that get in here?"

"I don't know," Wendy replied. "But get it out of here. Please!" She hoped her brother wouldn't act like a jerk, for a change.

"No problem," Brad said. He crossed to the mouse and picked it up by the tail. Wendy's eyes widened as she watched him lift it to his face. Brad opened his mouth as if he was going to pop it in. "Yum!" Brad said, smacking his lips. "Mousie for breakfast!"

Wendy shrieked. "Gross!" she shouted.

He dangled the mouse in front of her. "You didn't really think I was going to eat it, did you?" he teased.

Wendy glared at him in disgust. *Brothers.*

Brad laughed, then headed back out to the hallway carrying the dead mouse. "Meet you downstairs," he called over his shoulder.

"Ready for the gymnastics tryouts tomorrow?" Tina asked Wendy. They were changing from their leotards after Gymnastics Club.

"I'm as ready as I'll ever be," Wendy answered. She gave her combination lock a final turn and yanked open the locker.

"You're really good," Tina assured her. "I think you should make the team."

25

"Gosh, Wendy, I didn't know you had a fan club," said a familiar voice.

Wendy spun around. Nancy stood right behind her. Sneering, as usual. Suddenly Nancy reached past Wendy into the locker. "Well, look what I found," Nancy announced, holding up Wendy's blue T-shirt. "Anyone lose something?"

"Hey!" Wendy cried. "Give me that!"

"Who could this belong to?" Nancy went on. She laid the T-shirt across her chest, revealing the orange cat on the front. "Now, who would want such an ugly cat on the front of her shirt?"

"Cut it out, Nancy!" Tina yelled.

"Give me my shirt!" Wendy grabbed for the T-shirt. But Nancy stepped back and jerked it out of reach.

"Don't you ever wear anything but cat clothes?" Nancy waved the blue shirt over her head.

Wendy's face felt hot with anger. She could sense that all the other girls in the locker room were watching her. "Give it to me now!" Wendy shouted. She lunged at Nancy.

Nancy gave a fake shriek. "Oooh, don't scratch me, kitty!" she cried. "I'll give it back." She wrinkled her nose and held the shirt in two fingers, as if it smelled. Then she flung it backward over her head. Right into the shower area. It landed in a puddle of water. "Woops," Nancy said. "Too bad. I hear cats hate water." She laughed. Most of the other girls laughed, too. Then Nancy spun around and headed for the exit.

"You're going to get it, Nancy!" Tina yelled after her.

Wendy picked up the shirt, fighting back tears. Why is Nancy always so mean to me? she thought. What have I ever done to her?

"Come on, let's just go," Tina said. "We won't let her ruin our Friday night!"

Wendy borrowed a dry shirt from Tina, and they left the school. They always had a sleepover on Friday night. This week they were staying at Tina's house. Tina's mom always gave them hot chocolate and cookies before bed. Finally Wendy began to cheer up.

"Look at that cheetah!" Wendy exclaimed. "I can't believe anything could run so fast!"

"Awesome!" Tina said. "But my favorites are the tigers. They're coming up in just a minute."

The girls were working on a school project about the big cats. They lay on the leather sofa in the family room, watching a new nature video.

Tina's parents had already gone to sleep. Wendy and Tina were both in their pajamas. The best part about sleepovers at Tina's was that her parents let them stay up as late as they wanted. "As long as you let the rest of us get our beauty sleep," Tina's dad would joke.

As Wendy watched the graceful cheetah on the screen, she thought of something. "Where's Shalimar?" she asked.

"I don't know," Tina replied. Shalimar was Tina's

27

Siamese cat. He was a light tan all over, except for dark fur on his face, ears, tail, and paws.

Wendy loved to play with Shalimar. And Shal loved Wendy. Usually, whenever she visited Tina, Shal crawled over her. It was almost as good as having her own cat. Almost.

"You know, I haven't seen Shal the whole time I've been here," Wendy realized.

"You're right," Tina agreed. "Maybe he accidentally got shut in the basement. Put the movie on pause, and I'll go take a look."

Tina hopped off the sofa and Wendy clicked the remote. Then she lay back against the leather cushions. She gazed at the frozen image on the TV screen. A tiger in the video was suspended midair, all four of its legs stretched out in a graceful leap.

I can't imagine anything more beautiful than a cat, Wendy thought. Big or small.

Wendy yawned. She glanced at the clock on the mantel and saw that it was nearly midnight. She never got to stay up this late at home. Wendy took a deep breath and stretched her arms over her head. As she dropped her hands back to her lap, she realized that her fingers had begun to ache.

And then she remembered something. Something that scared her. Her fingers had ached last night, too. Right before her werecat dream.

Don't be silly, she scolded herself. It was just a dream. But her heart began to hammer as the ache in her fingers got worse.

It didn't happen, she insisted silently. Nothing happened.

Her skin began to itch.

I'm imagining things, she told herself. Trembling, she forced herself to look at her hands.

Her heart stopped.

Long tawny-colored hairs sprouted from her skin.

She wasn't imagining it.

It was happening again.

I'm turning into a cat, Wendy realized.

A *werecat!*

6

No! Wendy thought. This can't be happening!

She sat straight up. The itching began to spread. Cat hairs sprouted all over her body.

Stop! her mind shrieked. I don't want to turn into a cat!

She could feel her ears grow pointed. Her face began to twist. Her body started to shrink.

Wendy opened her mouth as wide as she could, trying to force her face to keep its human form. She tensed every muscle in her body. She clutched the leather sofa with all her strength. She had to stop the change!

But there was nothing she could do. She was more than half cat already.

It's true! Last night wasn't a dream after all. Wendy

gripped the sofa in terror. Her claws went right through the leather material.

Oh, no! What did I do? She stared at the torn sofa, then tried to pull away. She was stuck! Wendy tried again to free her claws. She pulled and twisted. The leather ripped loudly.

Still her claws were tangled in the leather. Finally, desperately, Wendy gave a sharp yank, and with another *rrrrippp!* her claws came free.

She stood in the middle of the torn sofa, panting from fear and effort.

"I can't find Shal anywhere," Tina's voice called from the hallway.

Tina! She couldn't let Tina see her like this!

Wendy leaped from the couch, streaked across the floor, and jumped out the open window.

Just as they had been the night before, all her senses were super-sharp. The moon was nearly full, and its light shone bright as day to Wendy's cat eyes.

Tina's going to wonder where I went, Wendy thought. But she had no choice. She couldn't let Tina see what she had become.

A wild animal.

A *werecat*.

Wendy's cat instincts began to take over. Her eyes darted back and forth as she watched tiny insects flittering in the moonlight. From far off she heard the sounds of mice burrowing in the ground.

The moon seemed to be calling to her—telling her to prowl. Wendy jumped up onto the fence that separated the backyards. She was eager to explore.

31

Exciting smells filled her nostrils. Where should she go first? Should she follow the delicious scent of mouse? Or maybe she should play with the moths.

An awful smell stopped her in her tracks. Dog! She glanced in the direction of the smell.

One of Tina's neighbors had a bulldog chained to a doghouse. Wendy perched above him for a moment. She knew him—he chased all the neighborhood cats. She dropped into the yard.

Wendy arched her back and hissed. The dog barked and lunged for her, but he was yanked back by the chain attached to his collar. Wendy stood just outside his reach and calmly washed her paws with her rough tongue. Doesn't the dopey dog know he can't reach me? she thought. The dog went crazy. He looked silly, tugging at his chain. And he barked really loudly.

This is fun! Wendy thought. Serves you right, picking on cats so much smaller than you.

When the lights went on in the house, Wendy bounded out of the yard. She went on prowling. The night breeze was cool on her fur and whiskers. Wendy stopped and reached her front legs up a pine tree. She plunged her claws into the bark and stretched. *Mmmmmmmmmm.* It felt as good as scratching a really bad itch.

A fluttering moth caught her eye, and Wendy chased it through an empty lot. The exercise made her body feel great. She leaped up onto the high fence where the moth had alighted.

Wendy's head whipped around to gaze at the house behind the fence. A strong, familiar scent floated to

32

her from the house and through the yard. It was Nancy's scent!

Wendy the werecat found Nasty Nancy's house.

An image of Nancy's sneering face filled her mind.

Nancy hates cats, Wendy remembered. She's allergic to them.

Wendy thought of Nancy's mean pranks and teasing.

I think I'll pay Nancy a little visit, Wendy decided. I'll see if she is allergic to werecats, too!

Wendy strolled along the top of the fence. She jumped into a leafy elm tree and climbed it to the top. Then she leaped into another tree and onto the roof of Nancy's house.

Her super-sharp nose told her she was directly above Nancy's room. Without even thinking about the height, she jumped down onto the windowsill below her. Good! The window was open a few inches.

Just enough space for Wendy—in cat form.

She pushed her head through the opening. She scanned Nancy's room. Posters of rock stars covered the walls. A pink teddy bear sat on the dresser. On the opposite side of the room Nancy lay sleeping. Her covers were pulled up around her ears.

Wendy bounded into the room. On a large armchair next to the bed she saw a neatly folded pair of pink leggings and an oversize purple sweater. Nancy's clothes for tomorrow, Wendy realized. Well, she thought, if Nancy doesn't like cat clothes, she'll really hate cats *in* her clothes!

Wendy leaped onto the chair. She made a nest of

the soft clothes, kneading them with her claws. She rubbed her body all over the outfit. She knew she was leaving her scent and cat hairs in the fabric.

She glanced over at Nancy sleeping peacefully. *You're in for a big surprise, Nancy,* Wendy told her silently. *I bet you're going to sneeze your head off tomorrow.*

Nancy still didn't wake up. Wendy watched her for a moment. Then an idea came to her.

Should I? she wondered. *Do I dare?* Wendy felt her werecat wildness tug at her. She approached the bed. Wendy gracefully leaped up beside Nancy. She waited a moment, making sure the movement didn't wake Nancy. But Nancy never stirred.

Nancy slept with two pillows. Wendy stepped carefully to the pillow Nancy wasn't using. Then she plopped down on top of it, rolling back and forth.

When she was done, she daintily walked beside Nancy and sat at the foot of the bed. It was so easy! So much fun!

Wendy was pleased with herself. She'd been very bold. Much bolder than usual! She began to groom herself. She licked her right paw and rubbed it across her face.

Suddenly Nancy stirred.

Wendy's paw stopped midair. She stared at the sleeping girl.

Then Nancy opened her eyes.

Wendy froze. What would Nancy do when she saw her?

34

Luckily, Nancy's eyes immediately scrunched up tight as she let out a humongous sneeze.

"AH-CHOOOOOO!"

Quickly Wendy burrowed between the sheet and the bedspread. She made herself as flat as possible.

"Ah-choo! Ah-choo!" Nancy sat straight up in bed. She reached for a tissue from the box on her bedside table. She sneezed again.

"I can't get a cold!" Nancy muttered. "I better shut the window." She climbed out of bed. Wendy peeked out from her hiding place and watched as Nancy crossed to the window. Nancy sneezed once more, then reached up and slammed the window shut.

Shut completely.

There wasn't a crack, an inch, any kind of opening at the bottom.

Wendy was trapped.

7

Wendy wriggled down to the end of the bed. *What was she going to do?* She tried to make herself smaller.

Nancy yawned and returned to bed. Wendy knew she would be discovered any minute. She was too large to hide very well.

Nancy sneezed again, then lay down. But a moment later she sat up again.

"Ah-choo! Ah-choo! Ah-choo!"

Nancy turned on her bedside lamp and reached for another tissue. But she must have noticed Wendy hunkered down under the covers.

"What's that lump?" Wendy heard Nancy say.

Then Wendy felt the blanket being pulled away. She stared up at Nancy.

Nancy stared back. Her eyes widened. "A cat!" she shrieked.

Wendy froze.

"How did a dirty cat get in my room!" Nancy cried. She jumped out of bed. "Get out! she shouted. "Out! Get out!"

I'd love to! Wendy thought. But how? She leaped to the floor and scurried under Nancy's bed.

"Get out!" Nancy yelled again. "Out! Ahhhh-choo!"

Wendy peered out from under the bed. She glanced around, searching for a way to escape. But all she saw was Nancy coming toward her. Waving an umbrella.

Wendy's ears flattened against her head and she hissed.

Nancy knelt down and shoved the umbrella in Wendy's face. Wendy easily ducked out of the way. Then Nancy had a sneezing fit. She dropped the umbrella and ran over to get more tissues.

Wendy watched Nancy standing by the bedside table. "The window!" Nancy exclaimed. "The stupid cat must have come in through the window." She yanked it wide open, then raced to the opposite corner of the room. "Now get out!" she ordered Wendy.

Happily! Wendy thought. In a flash Wendy streaked across the room toward freedom. With one fluid movement she leaped up to the windowsill and out into the night. She landed on a tree branch.

"Don't come back!" Nancy wailed.

Don't worry, Wendy thought, I won't!

As Wendy headed for home, she thought that it was fun to be so daring! As long as she never got trapped inside again.

She suddenly became aware that she wasn't alone. She glanced back to see a large black animal running swiftly in her direction.

Instantly Wendy's heart began to beat faster. Her fur began to puff out. She felt herself grow angry.

Hey! It can't come here, she thought. This is my territory!

Wendy wanted to fight.

No one comes onto my turf!

Wendy's sharp hearing picked up a low growl from the black animal. Wendy leaped up onto a garbage can and watched the black animal approach. It moved more slowly now. It crept along the ground, its eyes focused intently on something.

As Wendy peered down from her perch, she realized the black animal wasn't after her. It didn't know she was there. But it was stalking *something.*

Wendy's back arched when she recognized that the black animal was another cat. It was much larger than she, and black all over. Except for a white star on its forehead.

A white star.

The mark of a werecat.

It growled again. Then it lifted its head and gazed straight at Wendy.

Wendy stared into the glittering eyes of another werecat.

8

Wendy froze. She was face-to-face with another creature just like her.

Only much bigger.

But Wendy didn't care. Her fur puffed out in a challenge. All she could think was how much she wanted to fight the larger cat. That she had to drive it from her territory. She prepared to attack.

But the black werecat turned away. It began to creep along the ground again.

Wendy didn't take her eyes off the animal. What was it stalking? Wendy peered down the sidewalk. Then she saw it. A small striped alley cat. That was what the werecat was after, Wendy realized. The alley cat cowered by a Dumpster.

The werecat sprang. An instant later the horrifying

sounds of a vicious cat fight reached Wendy's ears. Somehow, the alley cat slipped away from its much larger enemy. It ran off, yowling in fear.

The black werecat's eyes darted up and down the street. Its tail flicked back and forth. Who's next? it seemed to be thinking.

Its eyes locked on Wendy's face.

"Mowwwwwwrr!" it howled in challenge.

"Mowwwrr!" Wendy called back.

The black werecat advanced toward her. A part of her wanted to stay and fight. But another part, the human part, was afraid. Knew she couldn't win.

The werecat sprang. It was so big, so heavy, it knocked over the garbage can.

Wendy scrambled to regain her balance. She found herself on the ground, looking up at the much larger cat. Its sharp fangs glittered in the moonlight as it moved in for the kill.

Wendy knew she was no match for the black werecat. Even though she wanted to fight, she forced herself to turn away. She streaked out of the alley. But she could still hear the black cat's footsteps, smell its scent.

Her house was two blocks away. Wendy picked up speed and raced into the street.

SCREEEEEEK!

She heard the squeal of brakes as a car swerved to avoid hitting her. She bounded through the neighbors' yards, flying over fences.

The black cat stayed right behind her.

At last she saw the familiar wall that surrounded

her house. Wendy leaped over the wall and into the yard. I'm home! she thought. I'm safe!

But the black cat leaped after her. Wendy could sense it snarling down at her from on top of the wall.

Her wall! Wendy's werecat senses were on full alert. She was furious. How dare that cat invade my yard? This is my home. Mine!

Wendy stopped running. She knew the other cat was much bigger, much stronger. But it didn't matter. Her instinct to defend her home was more powerful than her fear. She turned to face her challenger.

The black werecat was gone.

Wendy leaped back up onto the wall, sniffing the air. The scent of the werecat had vanished.

It was over. For now.

Wendy streaked back across the yard and up the old oak tree. She raced along the branches to her open window and jumped inside. She noticed the first pinks of dawn beginning to lighten the sky.

A moment later her skin began to itch and tingle. In less than a minute Wendy was in human form again.

She glanced down at her pajama-clad body. Her muscles ached all over. Her skin was scratched in half a dozen places. She was exhausted, relieved, and excited all at the same time.

Amazing! she thought. Being a cat is awesome! She thought about how daring she had been. She remembered teasing the dog and her visit to Nancy's house. She loved the way all of her senses were heightened when she was a cat. She felt so powerful.

Then she remembered the black werecat.

Wendy shuddered. That cat wanted to kill her. And it could have, she realized. Yet she had wanted to fight it. The danger didn't seem to matter.

I was out of control, Wendy thought. I was as wild as the other werecat.

Then she had to admit something—something terrifying. She was as wild as the black werecat because she was a werecat, too.

Something not human.

I have to stop changing into a werecat, she thought. But could she?

She didn't know what made her turn into a werecat in the first place. She had never even *heard* of werecats until the cat show. Until Mrs. Bast told them those stories.

Wendy gazed at herself in the mirror. An ordinary girl gazed back. There was nothing catlike or scary about her. She looked the way she always did: reddish-blond hair, pale skin, faint freckles.

She noticed the werecat charm glittering against her nightgown like a black diamond.

The charm.

Could it be? She thought back. This all started when she took the werecat charm from Mrs. Bast. The charm that Mrs. Bast had refused to sell her.

Maybe *this* was why. Maybe Mrs. Bast knew.

Knew that the charm would turn her into a werecat.

Wendy quickly reached up to unlock the clasp. The charm was beautiful, and she would be sorry not to wear it anymore. But she had to stop turning into a werecat before she got hurt.

Her fingers fumbled with the clasp. It seemed to be stuck. Frowning, she turned the chain around so the clasp was in front. Watching her movements in the mirror, Wendy continued to work the clasp.

It still wouldn't open.

Frustrated, Wendy tried to yank the necklace off over her head, but the chain was too short to make it over her chin. She yanked harder, but the chain wouldn't snap.

This is ridiculous, she thought. I have to get this clasp open!

She glanced around, looking for something to use. She spied a pair of scissors on her desk. She grabbed them and then, holding the scissors carefully, tried to snip through the chain.

It didn't work.

Wendy's eyes met her reflection in the mirror. She saw panic in them.

It's stuck, she realized with horror. The charm is never coming off!

9

"**D**on't panic," Wendy scolded her reflection in the mirror. There has to be a way to get the charm off. I'll ask Tina to help me, she told herself. She promised to be at the gymnastics tryouts today.

Wendy pulled on a black turtleneck with white kittens on it, then piled her hair up in a white scrunchie.

On the way to school for the tryouts, Wendy realized that Tina might be angry with her. After all, she had jumped out Tina's window last night and never gone back. What would she tell Tina? Wendy would have to come up with some reason why she had disappeared.

Wendy stood outside the gym and crossed her fingers for luck. "I wish I wish I wish I make the team," she whispered. Then she strolled through the swinging doors. She sat beside Tina on a bleacher.

"What happened to you?" Tina asked as soon as Wendy sat down. "I called your house, but nobody answered."

"I . . . uh, I was . . ." Wendy's mind raced, trying to think of a believable answer. She avoided Tina's eyes and gazed around the gym. Then she came up with the perfect excuse. "I was so nervous about the tryouts today," she lied. "All of a sudden I wanted to be in my own bed."

She smiled at Tina, but inside she felt terrible about lying to her best friend.

Tina gave Wendy's hand a quick squeeze. "You'll do great!" Tina told her. "I'm here to cheer you on."

"Thanks." One problem down, Wendy thought. How many more to go?

"Say," Tina interrupted Wendy's thoughts. "Before you left, did you notice Shalimar do anything strange?"

Wendy thought back. "No," she answered. "I didn't see Shal all night. Why?"

"The couch was ripped to shreds," Tina explained. "Boy, is Shalimar in trouble. My mom is so mad she locked him in the basement."

"Oh, no!" Wendy cried. "It wasn't Shalimar's fault!"

Tina looked surprised, and Wendy felt herself blush. "I mean . . . Shal couldn't have done it," she continued. Wendy wanted to tell the truth. She knew

Shalimar didn't rip the couch. *She* did. She felt so guilty.

"I know," Tina said unhappily. "I tried to tell my mom Shalimar would never do something like that, but she—"

Her words were cut off as Ms. Mason began explaining the rules of the tryouts. A moment later the door opened and Nancy rushed into the gym.

Wendy gasped. She was shocked by Nancy's appearance. Nancy looked terrible. Her skin was covered with red spots. Her red nose seemed raw and her eyes were swollen. Nancy rushed to take a seat in front of Wendy and Tina. As soon as she sat down, she sneezed.

"You're late, Nancy," Ms. Mason commented. "We almost started without you."

"I'm sorry," Nancy replied. "I—AH-CHOOO!" She pulled a tissue out of her bag.

"If you're sick, you shouldn't be here," Ms. Mason told Nancy gently.

"I'm not sick," Nancy objected hoarsely. "It's just allergies. I'm fine, honest. I—I—AH-CHOO!"

Wendy's mouth dropped open. She had no idea that allergies could be so bad! She felt terrible.

"Let's get started," Ms. Mason said. Wendy glanced at the nine other girls who were also trying out for the Shadyside Middle School team. She knew she might be in the top five, *maybe*, but that wouldn't be good enough. Only three girls would be chosen. And she had to be able to perform on the balance beam. Without falling!

"Wendy," Ms. Mason said. "You're first. Good luck!"

"Go for it!" Tina whispered. "It's in the bag."

Wendy smiled at Tina, then approached the mat. The floor routine was her best event. She was glad they were starting with it. She took a deep breath, tucked, and went into a forward roll.

Every cartwheel, every handspring, every flip was perfect. Wendy knew she had never performed better in her life. Her concentration never wavered. She remembered all the choreography. Her muscles responded exactly as she wanted. She was strong and graceful.

Graceful as a cat.

Even before she finished the routine, Wendy heard applause. Her face glistened with sweat. She came to her final position and grinned.

"That was excellent!" Ms. Mason exclaimed. "Debbie, your turn." Wendy returned to her seat, bursting with confidence.

Soon it was time for the final event of the tryouts. The balance beam.

Wendy had performed well so far. She knew she was one of the top four girls in the group.

She actually had a chance—a chance of making the team!

But now she had to face her toughest challenge. The balance beam.

Wendy's throat tightened as she walked toward the four-inch plank. You can do it, Wendy told herself. You're having a great day.

47

Wendy stood by the balance beam. She took a deep breath and glanced at the bleachers. Tina grinned and gave her a thumbs-up.

"Okay, Wendy," Ms. Mason urged her gently. "Whenever you're ready."

Wendy turned to the beam, then gracefully vaulted onto it. She held still for a moment, to sense her balance. She knew if she didn't balance correctly right from the beginning, she'd never make it to the end.

She began the routine. *Concentrate. Concentrate.* Involuntarily her eyes wandered to the floor. But for the first time ever, Wendy didn't feel afraid!

Maybe all her climbing as a werecat had cured her of her fear of heights. Wendy stopped worrying about how far down it was to the ground.

Halfway there, she thought. It was time for the front flip. Wendy tensed up. This is where she had fallen off so many times.

Wendy steadied herself, then went into the flip. She didn't even teeter! She nailed it!

Smiling broadly, she dismounted.

As Wendy returned to her seat, Ms. Mason nodded at her approvingly. Tina thumped her back. "You were amazing!" Tina cheered.

But Wendy knew it wasn't over yet. She was only third or fourth. Her spot on the team depended on how the rest of the girls did—especially Nancy. Nancy had always been better than Wendy on the balance beam. Wendy held her breath as Nancy began her routine.

But something was wrong. Nancy seemed unsure of her footing. Her face was still splotchy. Then, halfway across, she began to sneeze.

And sneeze.

Nancy fell off the beam.

Ms. Mason put an arm around her, but Nancy shrugged it off. She rushed back to her seat and buried her face in her hands. Wendy could see that she was crying.

Wendy felt awful. She knew how embarrassed Nancy must be. And even though Nancy always made fun of her, Wendy couldn't help feeling sorry for her.

Because Wendy knew it was her fault Nancy fell. I didn't know she would be so sick! Wendy thought. I never meant to ruin her chances for the team.

Then Ms. Mason made the announcement. "Top girl is Becky, then Sondra. Wendy is third."

"Congratulations," Tina exclaimed. "You did it!"

"Thanks," Wendy answered glumly.

"Hey, what's with you?" Tina asked. She and Wendy got up and headed for the locker room. "How come you're not thrilled?"

"I am," Wendy admitted. "I just feel bad for Nancy."

Tina stared at her. "After how mean she's been? Wow, Wendy. You're a lot nicer than I would be."

Wendy shrugged. She couldn't tell Tina she felt guilty. That Nancy fell off the beam because of her. That she had made Nancy sick.

That she was a werecat.

Wendy was more determined than ever to stop the transformation. She yanked off her gym shirt. "Tina, you've got to help me," she said. "You have to get this thing off me." She touched the cat charm around her neck.

Tina's eyes grew wide with surprise. "What are you doing with that?" she demanded. "I thought Mrs. Bast wouldn't sell it to you. Did you go back another day without telling me?"

"No," Wendy admitted. "I—I took it."

Tina's mouth dropped open.

"But I didn't steal it," Wendy added quickly. "I put five dollars in the tray."

Tina shook her head.

"But I think it's broken," Wendy continued. "And now I can't get it off. And I really, *really* have to." She turned around so Tina could get at the clasp.

"No problem." Tina fiddled with the necklace. It wouldn't open. "That's weird," she muttered.

"I told you," Wendy said. "Keep trying."

Tina tried pulling. She tried twisting. She tried her fingernails. She even tried her teeth. Nothing was working.

"This thing is really stuck," Tina said. "There's no way I can get it open."

Wendy's heart sank. She couldn't live with the necklace around her neck one more night!

"Then I have to go back to Mrs. Bast's booth and get her to open it for me," Wendy declared. "I have to."

50

Wendy and Tina rode their bikes to the cat show. The whole way Wendy worried. Mrs. Bast was going to be furious that she had taken the charm.

I can't think about that, Wendy told herself. I have to get rid of the charm. She didn't know of any other way to stop turning into a werecat. So no matter how mad Mrs. Bast was, Wendy would have get her to open the clasp.

Besides, she reassured herself for the hundredth time, I did pay for it!

The girls pedaled into the parking lot. Wendy glanced up at the building where the cat show was held. "Oh, no!" Wendy cried. She pulled her bike to a sudden stop.

"Whoa!" Tina exclaimed, swerving to avoid crashing into Wendy. "What is it?"

Wendy couldn't answer. She pointed at the empty store.

The cat show banner was gone!

"Uh-oh," Tina said. "Looks like they're gone."

"But—but—" Wendy sputtered. "They were just here!"

Wendy jumped off her bike, letting it clatter to the ground. She raced up to the front doors of the building. She yanked the handles.

The doors were locked.

Wendy peered in through the glass panes. All she saw was an empty room.

No tables. No booths. No cats.

No Mrs. Bast.

No one to open the clasp. No one to take back the werecat charm.

The cat show was over. Everyone was gone.

And now there was no way to find Mrs. Bast.

Wendy would be a werecat forever.

10

As soon as Wendy slammed through her front door, she raced over to the telephone table. She flung open the phone book and flipped to the Bs. But there was no Bast listed. Not in Shadyside. Not in Waynesbridge, the next town over.

Wendy hurled the phone book to the floor. I'll never find her, she thought. Never!

"Is something wrong, dear?"

Wendy glanced up. Her mother stood in the kitchen doorway. She wore a worried frown.

Wendy wanted to tell her mother everything. She even opened her mouth to start speaking. But then she stopped. What could she say? Her mother would never believe her. Believe that her "advanced" daughter turned into some kind of monster after midnight? No way.

Besides, Wendy felt terrible about taking the charm. She didn't want to admit she had done something so dishonest. Her mother would be disappointed in her.

No. Wendy couldn't say anything. She would have to solve the problem herself.

Her mother was still standing in the doorway. Wendy smiled. "No," she lied. "Everything's fine."

"Well, in that case I could use some help," Mrs. Chapman said. "I just made brownies and I need someone to lick the bowl."

"Hey, Mom," Wendy said, standing up. "It's a tough job, but somebody's got to do it."

Later that night Wendy carried a plate of brownies into the family room. Her mother and Brad were already sprawled on the couch, a huge bowl of popcorn between them. Mr. Chapman popped a video into the VCR.

"I got a movie I think you'll enjoy," he told Wendy. "It's called *Bell, Book, and Candle*. There's a Siamese cat in it."

"Cool!" Wendy commented. She liked Saturday-night movies with her family. And maybe a movie with an ordinary cat in it would take her mind off her *extraordinary* cat problems.

Brad rolled his eyes. "Bo-ring," he said. But he grinned and grabbed a handful of popcorn.

Wendy scrunched down on the floor with her back

against the sofa and the plate of brownies on her stomach. But once the video started, her mind began to wander.

To wonder.

Would she turn into a werecat again?

Of course she would. She never got the charm off. There would be no way to stop the transformation.

What would happen? Would the black werecat be out there? Would they fight?

"How do you like the cat?" Wendy's father's voice interrupted her thoughts.

"What?" For a moment Wendy didn't understand what he was talking about. Did he mean the black werecat?

Of course not, dummy, she told herself. Her father meant the cat in the movie. Pay attention!

"It's pretty," Wendy murmured. But she hadn't really noticed.

The video ended at a quarter to eleven. With a loud yawn Brad rose, stretched, and went up to his room. A few moments later Wendy's parents followed. Finally Wendy slowly climbed the stairs to her room.

Maybe it won't happen tonight, she thought.

But she knew it would.

Maybe, I can avoid the black cat. I know! I won't go out at all! I'll be safe that way.

That was the answer! Wendy was determined to stay inside. I can make my own decisions, even if I do turn into a werecat, she told herself firmly. I'll stay home.

Feeling more relaxed, she put on her nightgown and

55

turned out the light. But she didn't feel sleepy. She forced herself to lie down.

Bright moonlight shone through the curtains. Wendy glanced out the window. The moon was almost full. Only a tiny little sliver was dark.

Still she couldn't sleep.

The grandfather clock downstairs began to chime. DONG . . . DONG . . . DONG . . . DONG . . .

As it chimed for the twelfth time, Wendy felt the transformation begin.

"No," she moaned. "No!"

But there was no way to stop it. And Wendy changed much more quickly this time.

Was it because it was getting closer to the full moon?

In almost an instant the transformation was complete. Wendy's heart raced—in fear, in excitement.

"Mowwrr!" she exclaimed, standing on her pillow.

She was a werecat. A wild creature of the night. Ready to prowl! She leaped off the bed.

NO! she told herself. I won't go out tonight. I will stay here and go to sleep.

Wendy jumped back up onto the bed. She curled her tail over her face and shut her eyes.

But she was too restless. Her muscles ached for action. She wanted to prowl, to run, to chase bugs and mice.

NO! she told herself again. It's too dangerous. I won't go. I won't.

Trying to relax, she stood and stretched. She reached her paws far out in front of her and wiggled

56

her back end. Then she began to pace from one end of her bed to the other.

She couldn't stand it. She jumped off the bed, then up onto the dresser. Then she leaped back to the floor. Then she paced some more.

It was as if the night were calling to her.

Wendy forced herself to lie down again. Forced herself to listen to the human part of her mind.

But the werecat in her was stronger. Much stronger.

She couldn't fight it anymore. Her muscles seemed to be moving on their own. Suddenly she was out the window. She moved so fast, she was already on the ground before she realized what happened.

She stood on the moist grass, sniffing the air. She was out! Her senses reeled.

She picked up a movement nearby. A mouse! Wendy realized how hungry she was. She crouched down, preparing to stalk the mouse.

Then she heard a sound. A crunching sound of something moving in her direction.

Wendy whirled around.

There it was. A large, dark shadow moving toward her.

Stalking her.

For a moment the moonlight illuminated the dark shape. Just enough for Wendy to see a flash of white.

A white star.

It was the black werecat. Its yellow eyes glittered in the moonlight, staring straight at her.

Then it pounced.

Wendy twisted and sprang out of the way.

Her fur ruffled as the black werecat landed right behind her.

"Mowwwrr!" it screamed. It seemed furious it had missed her.

Wendy faced her enemy. The black cat's back was arched. It began to move toward her sideways. Its sharp teeth gleamed.

Wendy stood her ground. She puffed out her fur to make herself look as big as possible. Her ears flattened against her head. A low growl started deep in her throat.

So fast that Wendy never saw the movement, the black cat swiped her with its front paw. Wendy felt a sharp stab of pain as its claws sank into her leg.

"MEEEEEEOOOOWWWWWWRRRR!" Wendy howled. She tried to strike back, but the black cat was too quick. It easily avoided her reach. It crouched, ready to pounce again.

Wendy locked eyes with the black cat.

Then a tiny voice inside of Wendy told her to turn and run. That she should stop the fight right now. There was no way she could survive.

The black werecat lunged for her. But Wendy had already turned to run. Faster and faster, Wendy sped along the ground. Her back legs pumped together, pushing her into the air. Her front legs reached far out in front of her. The wind whistled by her face.

But as fast as she was, the black cat was faster. Its legs were longer. Its stride more powerful. With every step he drew closer.

Wendy cleared a large rock, then swerved to duck behind a bush. How could she lose him? She changed direction again. And again. Up ahead was a wall. It towered over her.

Wendy coiled herself, then leaped. Her front claws scrambled on the rough brick. She pushed hard with her hind legs. Then she hurled herself over the wall, into the alley beyond.

She heard a soft thump behind her. The black werecat was still on her trail.

Wendy tore down the alley. The black cat raced after her. Her leg began to throb where the black cat had scratched her. She felt blood trickling down, matting her fur.

And the black cat still got closer.

Wendy was running so hard her breath came in gasps. Her heart felt as if it would explode.

"Moowwwwrrr!" the black cat called in challenge.

Wendy didn't respond. She had to save her breath for running.

She knew she was running out of strength. Her only hope was to outsmart the other cat.

Suddenly Wendy swerved to the right.

Without thinking, she leaped straight up. She found herself clinging to a chain-link fence. She jumped into the yard below.

Wendy had no idea where she was. She'd never been in this part of the neighborhood. The moonlight cast sharp shadows as she searched desperately for some place to hide.

But there was no time. The black cat was on the fence. Wendy gazed up in terror as it crouched, ready to spring. Its mouth stretched wide as it howled again.

Again, Wendy glanced around, looking for an escape.

The black cat landed in the yard.

There was nowhere to run. She couldn't jump to safety. The black cat stood between Wendy and the fence. It approached her, hissing.

Wendy backed up.

Right into the base of a scraggly tree.

Wendy was cornered.

12

Wendy's entire cat body trembled. The black cat approached slowly. Closer. Closer.

Wendy's back arched even higher. She puffed out her fur. "Mowwwrrr!" Wendy cried. "Sssssttt!" she hissed.

The other cat stopped.

That was all the time Wendy needed.

Wendy whirled around. She leaped up onto the trunk of the pine tree. Using her sharp claws to hold on, she flung herself up the tree.

She heard the black cat behind her. She felt its weight shake the tree trunk.

Wendy climbed even higher. Into the small, skinny branches near the top. She hid her body in the shadows of the twigs and the pine needles.

The black cat was still after her.

But it had slowed down. It was a large animal. It had to be more careful climbing among the thinner branches.

Wendy remained completely motionless. The other werecat didn't see her!

But then the scratch on her leg began to throb. Instinctively Wendy licked it.

The black werecat's head whipped around in Wendy's direction. It had noticed the movement. It climbed closer.

Wendy crouched deeper into the pine needles. She couldn't climb any higher.

The black cat crept closer.

It was only a few feet away now. It gazed directly at her. It hissed.

Wendy shut her eyes. Waiting. Waiting for the attack.

But nothing happened.

She sensed a sudden movement. Her eyes popped open.

And she couldn't believe what she was seeing.

The black cat was climbing down the tree. Away from her.

She gazed after it until it disappeared.

Why didn't it attack? What could have scared it off?

Wendy noticed that the sky was growing lighter in the east.

The terrifying shadows had disappeared.

62

For the first time in hours Wendy wasn't afraid. She was safe now.

Except for one little problem.

Her skin began to itch. Her paws tingled. Her face twisted as her nose and mouth moved farther apart.

She was changing back!

In less than a minute Wendy had transformed into a human girl.

A human girl stuck at the top of a pine tree.

On one of the flimsy upper branches. A branch she could feel beginning to bend under her weight.

Wendy wrapped her arms and legs around it. When her heart stopped hammering, she glanced down.

It was so far . . . so far . . .

There was no way she could climb down!

13

Wendy gripped the tree branch as tightly as she could. It was no thicker than a broomstick.

And the ground was so far away.

She could feel the top of the tree sway in the wind. It had easily held a cat—even a werecat. But now Wendy was human. She was much too big for the small branch.

Stay calm, Wendy told herself. You have to get down!

Wendy forced herself to look down again. A wave of dizziness washed over her. The entire world seemed to spin.

I'm going to fall! she thought in a panic. She was up so high! Her hands began to sweat. Wendy's terrible fear of heights was taking over.

NO! Wendy ordered silently. Remember yesterday. Remember the gymnastics tryout. She had been strong. The balance beam was a snap. Being far off the ground had not bothered her.

You can do it.

Wendy forced her hands to relax their grip on the branch. Then slowly, cautiously, she moved first one hand, then the other to the tree trunk.

Then she eased her body off the branch, slid her feet down, and lowered herself to the branch below.

This next branch was sturdier, thicker. She felt a tiny bit safer holding on to it.

But she was still far above the ground. She had to keep going. She couldn't let herself relax.

She had more climbing to do.

Again, she held tightly to the tree trunk and eased down to the next lower branch, and then the one below that. She stopped and took a deep breath.

She reached out with her legs for the next branch.

And felt only air.

Her grip on the tree started to slip.

Her legs kicked back and forth in panic. Needles pulled at her nightgown. The dizziness returned.

Her sense of balance and strength vanished.

"No!" Wendy cried.

And then her foot struck something solid. Another branch. Carefully, she put her weight on it.

She leaned into the tree trunk to steady herself. She waited for her heart to go back to beating normally. But she knew she had to continue her descent.

Branch by branch.

It was getting easier. The farther down she went, the thicker and stronger the branches. The easier to hold on.

Wendy glanced down again. The ground was still far away. But she wasn't dizzy. She wasn't afraid.

Wendy stopped to untangle her nightgown from a cluster of needles. I'll just rest a minute, she thought. Her efforts had exhausted her.

She leaned against the trunk, pleased with her progress. And thrilled that her fear was gone.

Then she heard it.

The sound of wood splitting.

"No!" Wendy whispered.

With a loud CRACK! the branch Wendy was perched on split off from the tree.

"Nooo!" Wendy shrieked again. She scrambled toward the tree trunk and tried to grab on. She wanted to sink her claws into the tree, to keep from falling.

Her hands scraped on the rough bark. She couldn't hold on.

Screaming, Wendy fell.

14

Thud! A moment later she landed in the thick grass at the base of the tree.

Stunned, Wendy lay on the ground. Nothing seemed to be broken. Carefully she sat up. She was scratched, bruised, and sore, but not really hurt. Wendy blinked a few times and shook her head to clear it. No serious damage.

Wendy stood, shivering in the early dawn. She brushed herself off. Her nightgown was grass-stained and torn.

Her nightgown?

Yikes! What if someone sees me? Wendy thought. I have to get home—fast!

Wendy scurried out of the yard and into the alley. She tried to remember all the twists and turns she had taken when she was running from the black werecat. Luckily, it was very early Sunday morning. She didn't see another person all the way home. Finally she reached her house. She found the spare key under the flowerpot on the back porch, then quietly unlocked the kitchen door.

Good! No sign of her parents or Brad. They usually slept late on Sundays.

She tiptoed upstairs. Her arms and legs were covered with scratches. There was a larger gash on her forearm, where the black werecat had clawed her. After showering, Wendy smeared first-aid cream on her cuts. "I should have taken a bath in this stuff," she muttered.

She didn't know what to do with her torn and grass-stained nightgown, so she hid it in the back of her closet. Then she pulled on her jeans and a black sweatshirt. One of her few outfits that didn't have a cat on it.

This is it! Wendy thought. Being a werecat almost killed me! I have to stop it. Somehow!

She gazed at her reflection in her dresser mirror, glaring at the werecat charm. She tried to open the clasp. Of course, it was still stuck.

Wendy snuck down to the basement, where her father kept his tool kit. She found a pair of wire clippers. Holding them very carefully, she tried to cut through the chain.

It didn't work.

Wendy flung the wire clippers to the floor, fighting back tears of frustration.

I need help, she thought. I can't do it alone.

But who could help her?

Tina! Of course. Tina would help her.

Tina was her best friend. They always told each other everything. And Wendy felt terrible keeping such a big secret from her.

But would Tina believe her? I'll find a way to convince her, Wendy decided. Between the two of them, Wendy was sure they would find a solution.

Wendy felt better just knowing she was finally going to share her problem with Tina. After leaving a note for her parents, Wendy hopped on her bike and pedaled over to Tina's house. Tina's mom was already out in the garden, weeding the flower bed. Tina sat on the back porch, glumly staring into space.

"Hi," Wendy called. She left the bike in the yard and joined Tina on the porch. "You look upset. What's wrong?"

"My parents are still mad at poor Shalimar," Tina explained. "He's still locked in the basement."

"Because of the ripped couch?" Wendy asked.

"Yes." Tina sighed. "I told them he never came into the TV room that night." She shrugged. "But maybe he did. Maybe he sneaked in while I wasn't looking."

Go ahead, Wendy told herself. Tell Tina who really ripped the couch.

Wendy fought back her nervousness. "Uh, Tina? Shalimar definitely didn't rip the couch."

"How can you be sure?"

Wendy took a deep breath. Here goes. "Because it was me."

Tina stared at Wendy, then burst out laughing. "Anything to get Shal off the hook, right?"

"I'm serious," Wendy insisted. She glanced over at Tina's mom in the nearby flower bed. "Let's go inside. I have something important to tell you."

Still giggling, Tina followed Wendy into the house. "Okay, Wendy," she said as soon as they were inside. "What's up? Why are you acting so weird?"

Wendy wasn't sure what to say. She pulled the werecat charm out from under her shirt. "I think I know why Mrs. Bast wouldn't sell this charm to me."

"Because she's a wacko?" Tina joked.

"Because it's not just a necklace. It has special powers. And I think Mrs. Bast knew." She could see Tina was about to say something, but Wendy wouldn't let her. "Ever since I started to wear this charm," she continued, "I've been turning into a werecat."

Wendy took a deep breath. There. She said it. She gazed at Tina, wondering how her best friend would react.

Tina stared at her without saying a word. Then she exploded in a fit of giggles. "I knew there was something different about you lately," she gasped between guffaws.

"Tina!" Wendy cried. "I'm serious. I turn into a werecat at night. I—I'm covered with fur! I prowl the alleys! I—"

Tina was laughing so hard, she actually doubled over. "Stop it, Wendy! Let me catch my breath."

Wendy's mind raced. She had to make Tina believe

70

her! What could she say to convince her? But Wendy was having trouble concentrating. A noise in the dining room tugged at her attention.

It was a soft noise, a rustling noise. Wendy recognized it as a bird in a cage. It must be Merribel, the Barnes's pet bird. Wendy knew the birdcage was in the dining room by the window.

On the other side of the wall.

Wendy heard the soft fluttering of the bird's feathers as it groomed itself. How can I hear that through the wall? she wondered.

"You nut!" Tina exclaimed, shaking her head. "Wendy the werecat! That's a good one!"

"Right," Wendy murmured. She was barely listening. Her mind was filled with the image of the canary. She began to move toward the dining room.

The bird continued grooming. The sound of its beak stroking its feathers rang in Wendy's ears. I have to get to the bird, Wendy thought. As if she were controlled by an unseen force, Wendy found herself in the dining room in front of the birdcage.

The canary sat on a perch. Its beak moved swiftly across its feathers. Wendy carefully opened the cage door. The bird continued to groom.

It looks so soft, she thought. I'll just touch it.

The canary raised its head and gazed at Wendy. Slowly, as slowly as a stalking cat, Wendy slipped her hand into the cage. Her fingers closed around the tiny bird. She brought the bird out of the cage and held it up to her face.

The bird's warm scent filled her nostrils.

71

Mmmmmmmmmm. Delicious, Wendy thought. Just a taste, she told herself. Just a tiny little taste.

Wendy opened her mouth.

Then she stuck out her tongue and gently licked the bird.

"Wendy!" Tina's voice shrieked behind her. "What are you doing?"

15

Wendy whirled around. Tina stood in the dining room doorway, her eyes wide with shock. "I—I—nothing," Wendy stammered. "I'm not doing anything!" She glanced down at the canary in her hand. Its tiny heart pounded with terror. It struggled against her grip.

Tina began laughing again. "Sorry, Wen. Chomping Merribel still won't convince me that you're a werecat." Tina took the terrified bird from Wendy and locked it back in the cage. "Good try, though."

Wendy couldn't say anything. She was too stunned. I was actually going to eat the canary, she realized. Her werecat nature was getting stronger. It was beginning to control her, even during the day. Even in her human form.

Tina turned and smiled at Wendy. "If werecats really existed," she said, "you would be a great one. No one loves cats more than you."

Wendy sighed. Tina was not going to believe her. Tina wouldn't be able to help her. Face it, Wendy, she thought sadly. You're alone. All alone.

"I can always count on you to be a goof. Thanks for trying to cheer me up," Tina said. "I feel so bad about Shalimar. Hey, I have an idea," she continued. "Let's hang out with Shal in the basement. He's so lonesome down there."

Wendy felt even worse. That's my fault, too. Shal is being punished because of something I did.

She gave Tina a weak smile and then followed her down the basement steps.

"Shalimar!" Tina called. "Here, Shal!" She stopped on the bottom step. "That's weird," she said. "Usually I have to stop him from flying out of the basement the second I open the door."

Wendy glanced around the room. There was no sign of the Siamese cat. "Here, Shal," Wendy crooned. "Here, kitty, kitty, kitty."

"I guess he's hiding," Tina figured. "Something must have scared him."

The girls poked around the basement, searching behind boxes and under furniture.

Wendy spotted something beneath an old easy chair. She lay flat on her stomach. "Found him," Wendy announced. She reached for the cat. "Come on, boy," she urged.

74

Shalimar's blue eyes glittered at her. He wasn't moving. "Come on," she repeated. She stretched her hand toward him.

Suddenly Shalimar hissed and clawed at her. Wendy recoiled. "He scratched me!" she cried. Shalimar streaked across the basement and bounded up the stairs.

"He'll get out!" Tina shouted. "I left the kitchen door open!"

Forgetting about her scratched hand, Wendy scrambled up the stairs after Tina. Shalimar was a house cat. He never went outside.

When Wendy rushed into the kitchen, Tina had already cornered Shalimar by the sink. "It's okay," Tina said soothingly. The frightened animal's eyes darted back and forth.

Then they locked onto Wendy. Instantly he arched his back and hissed again. With a burst of energy he bounded out the kitchen door.

"What's wrong with him?" Tina wailed.

But Wendy was afraid she might know. Mrs. Bast's words echoed in her head: *"Werecats and ordinary cats are mortal enemies."* Shalimar used to love her. But now that Wendy was a werecat, he was terrified of her.

"Come on!" Tina shouted. "We have to get him back!" The girls raced out of the house. They searched the backyard.

"There he is!" Wendy cried. Shalimar was perched on top of the backyard fence. As soon as he spotted

75

Wendy, he leaped into the neighboring yard. Tina and Wendy rushed through the gate, calling to the cat. But Shalimar continued to run. He darted across Hill Street and through a large corner yard.

"He's headed for Fear Street," Wendy realized.

"If we don't catch him, he'll get run over!" Tina wailed.

Shalimar kept running. Wendy and Tina raced after the cat. When Shalimar reached Old Mill, he turned and streaked into another alley. Wendy, out of breath, arrived a moment later.

But the alley was empty.

"Where is he?" Tina wailed.

"Maybe he went into one of the yards," Wendy suggested. She glanced around the alley, trying to decide which way the cat might have gone. Then she spotted him.

"Tina," she whispered, "there he is." She pointed down the alley. Shalimar perched on top of a garbage can at the far end of the alley. He was licking his right paw.

"Oh!" Tina exclaimed. "He's hurt!"

"Shhh!" Wendy held a finger to her mouth. "We don't want him to take off again."

"Right," Tina agreed. They nodded at each other, then very slowly, very quietly, crept toward the cat.

Shalimar continued licking his paw. Tina and Wendy were halfway down the alley when a gate opened. An old woman wearing a dress with a cat on the front tottered into the alley.

"Look!" Wendy cried in surprise.

At the same moment Tina said, "It's Mrs. Bast!"

The old woman didn't seem to notice the girls. She strode quickly toward Shalimar. In one swift move she grabbed the cat and thrust him into the basket she was carrying. Then she disappeared around the corner.

"NO!" Tina shrieked. "She has Shalimar!" The girls sped to the end of the alley. They peered around the corner.

But Mrs. Bast was gone.

Tina slumped against Wendy's shoulder. She looked as if she were about to cry. "She stole him. Shalimar is gone forever."

"Don't worry," Wendy comforted her friend. "Mrs. Bast can't have gotten far. We'll find them. I promise."

Tina nodded. She took a shaky breath. "Okay. Which way?"

"You go that way," Wendy instructed, "and I'll go down the other block. We should be able to spot her." Tina nodded and began to jog down the street.

Wendy raced to the end of the block. She glanced all around. Bingo! "I found her!" she shouted to Tina. She took off after Mrs. Bast. A moment later Tina caught up with her.

"What if she won't give him back?" Tina asked, worried.

"Let's follow her. We'll think of something," Wendy reassured her.

And I'll think of a way to get Mrs. Bast to help me, Wendy thought.

77

Wendy felt Tina tug at her sleeve. "What is it?" Wendy asked.

Tina pointed to a street sign. "Uh, Wendy," she said nervously. "Look where we are."

Wendy glanced up. Fear Street. They were now following Mrs. Bast down Fear Street.

Fear Street wasn't like the other streets in Shadyside. It always seemed colder, darker. Enormous trees lined both sides of the street. Wendy shuddered. Those branches look ready to grab us, she thought. Strange shadows danced along the ground.

Figures, she thought. Of course this is where Mrs. Bast would lead them. Nothing had been normal since Wendy met the old woman.

"She lives here," Tina whispered. Wendy watched Mrs. Bast disappear inside a small shabby house.

Still carrying the cat in the basket.

"Come on," Wendy said. "Let's find out what she's up to." She gestured for Tina to follow her.

Wendy tried to quiet her pounding heart as she sneaked up to the house. She crawled across the porch and crouched below the window. Tina knelt beside her. Keeping her head low, Wendy peered through the dirty panes.

The room was dark and gloomy. Wendy spied an old purple sofa with the stuffing falling out and a large dining room table. As the girls watched, Mrs. Bast placed the basket in the center of the table.

"What's she going to do to Shalimar?" Tina wondered, her voice shaking.

"Don't worry," Wendy assured her. "We won't let anything bad happen to him."

Wendy gazed through the glass. Mrs. Bast stood over the basket. Wendy could see that Mrs. Bast was talking to herself but couldn't hear the words. The basket began to shake.

Mrs. Bast reached into a box on the table and pulled out jars and bottles. She lined them up by the basket, continuing to mutter. Then she lifted the lid of the basket, pulled Shalimar out, and set him on the table.

Holding the cat with one hand, Mrs. Bast picked up a large bottle with the other. She sprinkled white powder on the cat. Her lips moved rapidly the whole time.

Wendy sank back on her heels. A chill ran down her spine. Of course! It all makes sense, she realized with horror. Mrs. Bast is a witch!

The pieces fit together. The werecat charm. Wendy's transformation. The house on Fear Street.

The bottles must be filled with potions. Mrs. Bast must be putting a spell on Shalimar!

A loud yowl from inside the house interrupted Wendy's thoughts.

"She's torturing him!" Tina cried.

"We've got to stop her!" Wendy yelled.

The girls scrambled to their feet. Wendy yanked the door open and rushed inside. She had to save Shalimar!

"You let go of him!" she shouted at Mrs. Bast.

79

"Shalimar!" Tina called.

Mrs. Bast glanced up from the table. Her eyes were wide with surprise. Then they narrowed. She raised a long bony finger and pointed straight at Wendy.

"You!" Mrs. Bast growled.

16

"**Y**ou!" Mrs. Bast repeated. "It's you!"

"Mrs. Bast," Wendy began. But she didn't know what to say.

Shalimar howled even louder. He struggled in Mrs. Bast's grip, twisting his body in an effort to escape.

Mrs. Bast's eyes returned to the cat. "Stop that," she ordered.

The cat broke free. It leaped from the table, scattering bottles and jars. Wendy's hands reached out to keep the bottles from smashing to the ground.

"Shalimar!" Tina cried. "No!" Tina and Mrs. Bast grabbed for the cat at the same time. It ducked out of reach, then bounded to the top of a tall bookcase.

Wendy glanced up. The cat gazed down at them, then began to wash its face.

"Wendy!" Tina exclaimed. "Its not Shalimar. Look—it has one brown eye. Shal's eyes are both blue."

Wendy peered at the cat. Tina was right. The cat looked exactly like Shal except for its eyes.

"Look what you've done," Mrs. Bast scolded. "Look at this mess." She began to pick up the bottles and jars that had fallen. Wendy tried to help, but Mrs. Bast stopped her. "Haven't you done enough already?" she scolded. "I know who you are. You're the girl who stole the werecat charm."

Wendy's face flushed with embarrassment. Mrs. Bast was right to be angry with her. "I'm sorry," she said. "But I did pay for it. I didn't really steal it."

"Hmmmph," Mrs. Bast grunted.

"And I'm here to return it," Wendy continued. Now, finally, she'd be able to get rid of the necklace. "But I can't get the clasp open."

Mrs. Bast gazed at Wendy for a long moment. Wendy wondered what the old woman was thinking.

Mrs. Bast shook her head. "Sorry. But you'll never get that charm off. Never."

17

Wendy stared at Mrs. Bast, horrified. "Did you say—did you say I'll *never* get this charm off?" she repeated. Her voice shook.

"That's right," Mrs. Bast said firmly. "It will never open." She paused, then leaned very close to Wendy. "Unless you find the secret clasp."

Wendy blinked. "The secret . . ." Wendy wasn't sure she had heard correctly.

"It's very cleverly hidden," Mrs. Bast explained. "Come over to the mirror. I'll show you."

Dazed, Wendy followed the old woman to a large dusty mirror hanging on the wall. She stood silently as Mrs. Bast pulled the clasp to the front. "Now, you see this?" Mrs. Bast asked. Wendy nodded. "It looks like a regular clasp. It looks like all you have to do is unhook it. But . . ." Mrs. Bast's eyes twinkled. "Instead you have to turn it clockwise, then pull it through the cat charm. Like this."

With nimble fingers Mrs. Bast released the catch. The necklace opened. Wendy was free!

"No wonder we couldn't get it off," Tina said.

A wave of relief swept over Wendy. It was over. The charm was off. She would never be a werecat again!

"Oh, Mrs. Bast, thank you! Thank you so much!" she cried.

"You shouldn't have taken the necklace," Mrs. Bast said sternly.

"I know." Wendy hung her head, ashamed. "I know I should never have done it. But I wanted it so badly. It was as if I couldn't help myself."

Mrs. Bast nodded. "I feel the same way about the charm. I never meant to sell it. It's from my personal collection. I don't even know how it wound up in the five-dollar tray."

"Please, take it back!" Wendy said. "And keep the five dollars, too."

Mrs. Bast smiled, then slipped the charm into her pocket. Wendy wondered if the old woman knew about the power the charm had. Well, she figured, if Mrs. Bast really is a witch, maybe she doesn't mind turning into a werecat every night.

Three nights had been enough for Wendy!

"Now, explain yourselves," Mrs. Bast demanded. "Why were you two girls following me?"

"We thought you had my cat, Shalimar," Tina explained. "We saw you pick him up in the alley."

"Or we thought we did," Wendy added.

"Don't you know all Siamese cats resemble one another?" Mrs. Bast said. She glanced up at the cat still perched on top of the bookcase. "Meet Magnolia," she told the girls, waving at the cat. "One of my regular clients."

"One of your . . . whats?" Wendy asked. What was Mrs. Bast talking about?

"Clients," Mrs. Bast repeated. "I'm a cat groomer. Didn't you know?"

"How would we know?" Tina asked.

"I just assumed girls who are so interested in cats would have heard of me," Mrs. Bast said indignantly. "I use my house as a grooming parlor."

Wendy tried to understand what Mrs. Bast was saying. Could it be true? Could Mrs. Bast be an ordinary woman, and not a witch after all?

"Why were you sprinkling powder on the cat?" Wendy asked.

"Why, to clean her coat," Mrs. Bast replied. "If you sprinkle a little cornstarch on a cat, it will absorb dirt. A free grooming tip." She winked at Wendy.

Wendy almost laughed out loud. She'd been so silly! Thinking Mrs. Bast was a witch! It was because of that stupid charm. But the werecat nightmare was over.

"Thanks again, Mrs. Bast," she said cheerfully. "And we'll tell all our friends what a great cat groomer you are!"

Wendy skipped out of Mrs. Bast's yard. Tina followed slowly. She stared down at the ground.

"Tina, what's wrong?" Wendy asked. Then she realized—Shalimar! Wendy was so thrilled about getting rid of the werecat charm that she had forgotten about the missing cat. Tina must feel terrible, Wendy thought. They still hadn't found Shalimar, and they had lost his trail completely.

"Come on," Wendy declared. "Let's keep looking."

They retraced their steps back to Tina's house, calling his name, searching the alleys. No luck.

When they entered Tina's backyard, Wendy could see Tina fighting back tears. "What if we never find him?" Tina asked sadly.

But Wendy was too relieved and happy to believe anything bad could happen to Shalimar. "Don't even think that!" she scolded her friend. "We'll put up posters, we'll call the animal shelter, we'll—"

Tina interrupted her. "Look!" she cried. She pointed to her back steps.

There he was. Sleeping peacefully.

"Shal!" Tina raced over to her pet. "Oh, Shal, are you all right?" She hugged him tightly to her. He gave a little mew and a sleepy yawn.

"Okay, Shal, into the house," Wendy called. She opened the kitchen door. At the sound of Wendy's voice, the Siamese wriggled out of Tina's arms and streaked into the house. He raced down into the basement.

"Whoa!" Tina exclaimed. "I never saw him go into the basement on purpose before."

"He's never been outside before," Wendy reminded her. "He's probably still scared."

And I know just how he feels, Wendy thought. It can be scary being a cat!

She smiled. That was all behind her now.

That night Wendy sat at her desk working on her homework. But her mind wandered, thinking over the strange events of the past week.

So werecats really exist, she thought. It wasn't just a story.

Now that it was over, she could admit how much she enjoyed being a cat. There were many scary things about life as a werecat, but she was glad it happened.

She loved being able to see in the dark. Her cat senses made everything exciting. The prowling, the roaming—it was all thrilling. She especially loved her cat confidence.

But she hated feeling out of control. Each time she transformed she became wilder.

And the black werecat! It almost killed her. It probably would have, the next time.

But there wasn't going to be a next time.

Wendy got up and gazed out the window. The full moon was rising high above the old tree in her yard.

Full moon. Mrs. Bast said the werecat was wildest at the full moon. And, Wendy remembered, once the werecat experienced the first full moon, the human and the werecat are completely blended. There is nothing human in the werecat, and the werecat's instincts come out even during the day.

Wendy shuddered. She was so glad she wouldn't transform tonight.

Wendy glanced into the yard. It was a perfect night to prowl. She could almost feel the soft grass beneath her paws, sense the mice scurrying in the bushes. . . .

No! she ordered herself. Stop thinking like that. It's over! She sat back at her desk and finished her homework.

Finally Wendy shut the book. She yawned and stretched. These last few days had been exhausting. She would go to bed early tonight.

She put on her nightgown, then opened the window to let in the fresh night air. Then she lay down and was soon fast asleep.

It seemed like only moments later that Wendy awoke. The full moon was high in the sky. Its light streamed in, illuminating the room almost like daylight.

Why is it so bright? Wendy wondered. She remembered how bright the moon seemed when she had been a werecat. Panic rose in her chest.

It's just because the moon is full, she told herself. You aren't wearing the charm. You won't transform again.

She punched her pillow and cradled her head in it. She turned and twisted, trying to find a comfortable position. She couldn't relax.

Why am I so restless? Her whole body felt tense, alert. Her arms and legs tingled.

"No," she whispered. "It can't be."

Her teeth and hands began to ache. Her skin started to itch.

"No," she moaned. "I'm imagining it."

She sat up in bed. "I'm not . . ." she whimpered. "I can't . . ."

Shuddering, she stared down at her hands.

Her fingernails looked unusually long. And curved.

Wendy couldn't tear her eyes away. She watched the tawny hair sprout from her hands.

She wasn't imagining things.

And it wasn't over.

She was turning into a werecat again.

18

"**N**o!" Wendy cried. "I won't let it happen!"

But the thick fur kept growing.

I'm dreaming! she thought desperately. I must be. The charm is gone. I'm a normal human girl.

She leaped off the bed and rushed to the mirror.

Her eyes turned green. Her ears moved to the top of her head.

She backed away from the mirror, then raced to the window. She slammed it shut. It's the moon, she thought. I have to hide from the moonlight. She ducked into her closet, pulling it closed behind her.

In the tiny space her harsh breathing sounded loud and ragged. She felt her heart hammering. And she felt the transformation taking place.

There was no way to stop it.

A moment later Wendy bounded out of the closet. As a werecat.

She leaped up onto her dresser. Trembling with fear, she once again faced her reflection in the mirror.

A fierce animal gazed back. A tawny-colored cat with a white star on its forehead.

NO! NO! NO! screamed in her brain. It wasn't the charm, Wendy realized. It was *her*. She was truly a werecat.

She was terrified of what might happen. What she might do as a werecat. She had so little control. She had destroyed Tina's couch. She got Shalimar in trouble. She hurt Nancy. She hurt herself.

And she knew that the black werecat was out there. Waiting for her.

Then I won't go out! Wendy decided. I will fight my werecat instincts. I will stay safe inside.

She glanced at the window. It was shut tight. Good, she thought with satisfaction. There was no way she could get out.

Wendy jumped off the dresser and leaped onto her bed. She curled into a ball on the pillow. She was determined to go to sleep. When I wake up, I'll be a normal girl again, she told herself. Human.

But as hard as Wendy tried to keep her eyes shut, she couldn't. The pull to go out was too strong. Images filled her mind, insects and animals, wonderful scents and places to explore.

Fight it, she commanded silently.

She had never felt so restless in her life. Her body actually began to twitch.

91

She rose from the pillow and paced the room. She jumped to the floor, up to the dresser, back to the floor. Over and over.

And with every step the desire to go outside became stronger.

I'll just peek out, she thought. That will be enough. I just want to see what's out there.

Wendy landed lightly on the windowsill. She peered through the glass.

The oak tree swayed in the wind. Even though the window was shut, Wendy's senses were aware of scents on the breeze. She could see insects flitting in the bright light of the full moon.

Wendy ached to be outside. But she knew she wouldn't be safe.

Suddenly her body tensed. A movement caught her attention.

It was a dark shadow, creeping along the large branch just outside her window.

A moment later the shadow filled the entire window.

In the center of the shadow were two glittering yellow eyes.

19

The yellow eyes vanished.

And so did all of the human girl in Wendy.

Furiously she swiped at the closed window. How dare that werecat come here? To my house!

It knew she was inside. It had been stalking her.

Now it was waiting. Waiting for her to come out.

There was a tiny part of Wendy that knew the black werecat was much stronger than she, much more powerful.

She didn't care.

She was in the grip of the full moon, the wildest time for the werecat. Her tail twitched, the tip flicking back and forth.

I must get out! I have to protect my territory from the black cat!

Wendy paced along the windowsill. She nudged her nose along the bottom of the window, searching for a crack, a way out.

Frustrated, she leaped to the floor. A movement across the room caught her eye. A gnat! She bounded across the floor in pursuit of the insect. But her leap was too wild. She crashed into the dresser.

She landed, shook herself, and gazed around the room, searching for the gnat. She sensed it above her. Wendy jumped up onto the dresser. She glanced around—and saw another cat!

Wendy's fur puffed out. Her back arched. The cat had sandy-colored fur like her. And had a white star on its forehead. Wendy hissed and spit at the strange cat.

The other cat arched and hissed back.

How did the cat get into her room? Wendy had to fight it. Drive it away. She lunged at it, her claws and fangs ready to rip it apart.

SKRREEEKKK!

Her claws scraped against something hard and smooth.

Wendy stepped back.

The brown cat retreated.

Wendy opened her mouth in a challenging cry.

The other cat's mouth opened, too.

Wendy stared at the intruder. Then she sat down and curled her tail around her legs. The other cat did the same. And now she realized that the other cat wasn't real. It was her reflection, gazing back at her from the mirror.

She was shocked by how wild she had become.

The full moon. The challenging black werecat. Even her own reflection. They all made her werecat instincts stronger.

She wanted to roam, to stalk, to—

"Moooowwwrrr!" A distant cry from outside pricked Wendy's ears. She recognized the voice of the black werecat. It was calling her. Calling her to battle.

She had no choice.

Trembling all over, Wendy leaped onto her bed. She crouched, getting ready. With a piercing yowl, she sprang into the air.

Straight toward the window.

The closed window.

20

CRAASSHHH!

Wendy's body flew through the air. The window shattered. Glass flew everywhere, sparkling in the moonlight.

Wendy easily twisted in the air.

WHUMP! She landed on her feet on the grass below the tree. She shook herself to get rid of the shards of glass. Then she licked her shiny fur.

She was fine. Not a scratch on her.

And she was out!

But where was the black werecat? It had been calling to her. Calling her to fight.

Now there was no sign of it.

Maybe it had been scared away when she crashed through the window.

Good, Wendy thought with satisfaction. This is my yard. My territory. She flattened her ears against her head and yowled. Mine!

It was already late. The moon was nearly setting.

But there was still plenty of time to prowl. Time to hunt. Time to find the black werecat.

She had to settle things with the other werecat. Had to show it whose territory this was.

Wendy sniffed the ground, searching for the scent of the other cat. Even though the moon was low, her sharp eyes revealed everything in the yard. Insects crawled through the grass. A moth fluttered against the porch. A gopher snake hunted beneath the white rosebush. But nothing would distract her from her mission.

To find the black werecat.

Wendy jumped onto the back wall. She stalked from one end to the other, searching, searching.

But there was no sign of her prey.

Had the black cat run away? Was it afraid of her?

Wendy puffed out in pride. She would teach the werecat a lesson. She would find it and teach it to stay away from her home.

Wendy lifted her nose into the breeze.

There it was. The faint, familiar scent.

Wendy's fur bristled. She leaped down into the alley. Crouching low to the ground, she streaked along, moving quickly, stealthily toward the scent.

As the scent became stronger, Wendy knew she was getting closer. She noticed something strange about the scent, something different. It was definitely the black werecat. But it somehow smelled . . . bigger? Stronger.

How could that be? Wendy wondered. But she couldn't think about that. All that mattered was challenging the black cat.

Wendy continued to follow the scent. It led her down to the end of the alley.

The scent was much stronger here. The scent of the black werecat and . . . something else.

But what?

Wendy held perfectly still, sniffing, listening. She picked up the sound of movement just around the corner.

Was it the black werecat? Was it coming to find her?

Now, Wendy's brain screamed. The last challenge. The final showdown!

Bracing herself for battle, Wendy whipped around the corner.

There it stood, its back arched. The black werecat.

Wendy gasped.

A cry caught in her throat!

Her eyes widened in shock when she saw what else was waiting around the corner.

21

Wendy's back went into a high arch. Her tail puffed up to twice its size.

The black werecat was not alone. Just behind it were two other cats. One dark brown, one tawny gold. Each with a white star on its forehead.

Two more werecats!

They were even larger than the black werecat.

And Wendy was their prey!

With a scream of terror Wendy turned and streaked back up the alley.

With answering cries, the three werecats ran after her!

Wendy never ran so fast in her life!

She shot like a bolt of lightning through the night.

Back home. Home to safety. She leaped up onto the wall that surrounded her yard.

The three cats were right behind her.

Trembling, Wendy stood her ground. She paced the top of the wall. She howled out a warning. *This is my territory, Go away!*

The three werecats stopped. They stared up at Wendy from the grass below.

And then all three huge cats jumped up. They landed gracefully on top of the wall.

Wendy leaped to the ground. She raced toward the oak tree.

If she could only make it to her room. If she could only make it back inside!

But the largest cat, the brown one, was too fast. It bounded between Wendy and the tree.

Wendy stopped short. She glanced around wildly, searching desperately for a place to hide, to climb. To escape.

The brown cat was ahead of her. Then Wendy sensed the black werecat stalking her, sidling up beside her.

A movement behind Wendy made her whirl around. The golden cat was also moving toward her. Its fur stood out like a halo.

Wendy was surrounded.

It's over, she thought in despair. It's all over.

22

Wendy puffed her fur out even more. She hissed and spat at her enemies.

She would not give up without a fight.

The cats came closer. Closer.

The golden cat was only inches away.

It opened its mouth. Its long, sharp fangs gleamed in the moonlight.

It lunged for her neck.

Wendy shut her eyes in terror. The gold cat was going to kill her!

An instant later Wendy felt a strange, rough stroke on her cheek.

Her eyes snapped open.

She stared at the gold cat in shock. It was licking her face. Then it snuggled up to her. It began to purr.

Wendy couldn't believe it. What is going on?

There was something familiar about the gold cat's scent, she realized. There was something familiar about the other werecats, too.

Wendy gazed at the black and the brown cat as they approached her. They weren't hissing or spitting. Their ears weren't flat against their heads anymore. Their tails stood straight up in friendly interest.

Wendy glanced around, puzzled. The yard was becoming lighter. The moon had set while she was running from the other werecats. Now the sun was beginning to rise.

Wendy felt a tingling throughout her body. The transformation back into human form was starting.

I have to get back to my room, Wendy thought.

She struggled to get away from the golden cat. But Wendy had only gone a few steps when the large brown cat once again jumped in front of her. Wendy tried to get around it.

It pounced.

The biggest of the cats knocked her to the ground. Before Wendy could pull herself up, the brown cat placed its heavy paw on her neck.

It held her firmly down. Wendy couldn't move.

Now the two other cats crept over.

Too late, Wendy realized the cats had only been playing with her. The way she had played with the mouse.

She was no match for the three of them.

And now they were going to finish her off.

23

The werecats closed in.

Wendy lay trapped under the enormous brown cat's paw. She was captive inside their circle. She shut her eyes in terror.

What will happen if I transform now? Wendy thought. What will these werecats do to a human?

She felt her face twist. The itchy feeling covered her body. Her hands ached as her paws turned back into hands with fingers.

The huge cat let go of her. A sense of relief flooded through Wendy—maybe the other werecats ran away.

She cautiously opened one eye. Then the other.

She gasped!

The three other werecats were transforming, too!

Fascinated, Wendy watched their fur shrink into their skin. Their faces shifted around and their ears changed shape. Their claws disappeared and turned into fingernails. And the whole time they were growing larger, becoming human again.

Suddenly Wendy felt afraid. These werecats were people, too—strange people who turned into monsters every night.

Who are they? Wendy wondered. What will they do now?

She jumped to her feet and edged toward her house. She had to get inside before they saw her as a human girl! Wendy turned to run.

A hand grabbed her wrist and spun her back around.

Wendy stared into three familiar faces.

Her mother. Her father. And Brad.

Wendy's mind raced. I must be dreaming. This can't be real. Can it?

"W—Wh—" Wendy stammered. She couldn't get any words out.

"Wendy," her mother said gently. Her fluffy blond hair looked golden in the dawn light.

Brad brushed his long black hair out of his eyes. Her father ran a hand through his thick brown hair.

The golden werecat. The black werecat. The large brown werecat.

"Mom!" Wendy cried at last. "Brad! Dad! I don't believe it!"

Wendy's mother smiled. "We're a little surprised, too."

"Man, Wendy," Brad said. "You're a lot tougher than I thought. Cool territorial cry you gave." He grinned at her.

Wendy still felt confused. "But—" She had so many questions, she didn't know what to ask first. "I thought it was the werecat charm. But then I still transformed. Even after I gave it back to Mrs. Bast."

Her parents glanced at each other. "There was a werecat charm in our family once," her mother said. "But it was lost ages ago. This Mrs. Bast must have found it somehow."

"You see," her father added, "your ancestors have been werecats as far back as anyone can remember."

"We were going to tell you, sweetie," her mother told her. "But we were waiting for the right time. We didn't expect you to change so early."

"Besides, squirt," Brad added, "you weren't allowed up after midnight!"

"Hey, is this why you never let me have a cat?" Wendy guessed.

Her father nodded. "It's why you've always been drawn to them," he explained. "But we couldn't have one in the house. No ordinary cat can live among werecats."

"They become our enemies," Brad said in a fake spooky voice.

"I didn't like that part," Wendy admitted. "All that fighting. And I got so wild."

"Everyone has trouble with that at first," her mother reassured her. "But soon you'll learn to control your werecat nature."

"Don't worry," her father added. "Now that you know, we'll help you. Teach you the werecat ways."

They began heading toward the house. "And Wendy," Brad piped up, "if you thought prowling the alleys was fun, wait until I take you hunting in the Fear Street Woods. I'll show you all the best spots."

Wendy came to a sudden stop. "Why did you attack me?" She glared at Brad accusingly. "You almost killed me!"

Brad hung his head. "Sorry," he said sheepishly. "But I didn't know it was you."

"It's true, Wendy," her father said. "None of us did. No one in our family has ever changed at such a young age."

"I was almost fourteen when I transformed," Brad said. Wendy thought he sounded a little jealous. "Maybe it was the charm," he suggested. "Maybe that made you transform early."

"Maybe," Wendy's mother said with a smile. "But after all, Wendy has always been advanced for her age!"

ARE YOU READY FOR ANOTHER WALK
DOWN FEAR STREET?
TURN THE PAGE FOR A TERRIFYING
SNEAK PREVIEW.

R.L. STINE'S

GHOSTS OF

FEAR STREET

HOW TO

BE A

VAMPIRE

Emily whirled around. "I'm not falling for any more of your stupid tricks, Andrew!" she warned him.

Andrew scanned the trees—and saw the figure.

A figure in a long, sweeping cape.

The dark form slid out from behind a giant oak, inching closer and closer.

"There he is!" Andrew shouted. "Behind you!"

"Yeah, right." Emily stood in place with her hands on her hips.

The figure stepped silently up to Emily.

It hovered behind her.

"Emily, I'm not kidding." Andrew's voice quivered. "Run!"

Emily shook her head in disgust.

The figure raised his dark hands.

"Emily! Run!" Andrew pleaded.

Too late.

Andrew watched in horror as a pair of twisted fingers lunged for Emily's neck.

Emily screamed.

Her cries pierced the chill October air.

She twisted in the dark figure's grasp, struggling to free herself. "A vampire!" she cried. "Help me, Andrew!"

Andrew didn't move. He stared at the caped figure. At his long fangs dripping with saliva.

"Andrew, do something!" Emily shrieked.

"Vhat a screamer you are," said the creature of the night. He released Emily from his grasp. He spit—and his fangs flew into his black-gloved hand.

Andrew fell to his knees—and laughed.

"Oh, man!" he cried. "That was awesome, T.J.!"

Emily smoothed her hair. She centered her pearl necklace.

"You immature creeps," she growled. "You are so pitiful. You act like two-year-olds!" With that she whirled away from them. She marched toward the park exit.

"Oh, man!" Andrew said again. He watched his sister stomp angrily past the baseball diamond. "I wish I had that on video."

"You'd think she'd be used to it by now," T.J. said,

shaking his head. "But she falls for our pranks every time."

T.J. picked up his backpack from behind a tree. He untied his cape and took it off. He folded it carefully and tucked it into the backpack. He placed his plastic fangs in their spot in his pen-holder compartment.

Andrew admired T.J. When he pulled a prank, he went all the way. T.J. wasn't very tall. In fact, he was short and stocky. But he'd slicked back his hair with some of his older brother's mousse, and somehow managed to look like a full-size vampire.

Andrew admired T.J. for another reason. He was loyal to vampires. Andrew loved all kinds of monsters. Werewolves. Mummies. Ghouls. Swamp things. But T.J. stuck to vampires. He knew everything about them. He was a specialist.

"This was better than when we scared Emily with the King Kong mask," T.J. said. "It was even better than the time we slimed her."

Andrew grinned, remembering. He'd gotten in trouble for that one. Mega trouble. But it was worth it. And Emily deserved it. She kept making fun of one of his monster books. *Alien Slime from Mars*. Then one night, he and T.J. arranged for her to see some slime for herself. Andrew giggled, thinking about how she stared in horror as green goo dripped down from her light fixture. How it plopped right down on her head. He was pretty sure that, for a second, Emily believed it was alien slime from Mars.

The next morning, Andrew jolted awake. Somebody was screaming! Screaming his name! He sat straight up in bed.

"Huh?" he cried.

"Get up!" Emily shouted from the doorway of his room. "Now!"

With a groan, Andrew fell back onto his bed. He burrowed deeper under his covers. He shut his eyes. Clearly Emily had not forgiven him for the vampire prank.

"Turn off your stupid alarm!" Emily shouted.

Alarm? Oh. That's what was going *beep, beep, beep.* Andrew had been dreaming that a vampire was knocking on his window. The vampire said *beep, beep, beep.* Finally Andrew got up and opened the window for him. What a stupid dream. A *beeping* vampire.

Still half asleep, Andrew reached a hand out from under his blanket. He waved it in the direction of his clock. At last he made contact. He hit the alarm button. The beeping stopped.

"We are going to catch the first bus this morning, Andrew," Emily announced. "If you aren't downstairs in fifteen minutes, I'm leaving without you. I don't care what Mom says."

Andrew heard his sister stomp down the stairs. If Emily left by herself, their mom would have a fit.

Shadyside Middle School was pretty far away from their development—but very close to Fear Street. Close to the Fear Street Cemetery. Scary things happened there. All the time. If you believed the stories . . .

Andrew believed them. He knew that on Halloween, ghost kids rose from their graves. They tried to get real live kids to play a game with them. The game was called Hide and Shriek. The object of the game was to take the live kids back to the grave!

And then there was Miss Gaunt. She used to be a substitute teacher at Shadyside Middle School. Before she died, that is. Now she haunted the cemetery. She was always out searching for new students to teach—forever!

Mrs. Griffin always told Andrew that they were only stories—that she did believe there was any truth to them. But still, she liked Andrew and Emily to travel to and from school together.

With a groan, Andrew made himself open his eyes. He needed more sleep. Much more sleep. He wished he hadn't stayed up reading so late the night before. He wished he could sink back onto his soft pillow again. And close his eyes . . .

He jerked his head up. Any minute now, Emily would be back, screaming at him. He pushed himself up on one arm. Ow! His elbow hit the corner of his book. The one he'd been reading half the night. *Running with Werewolves*. Boy, what a great story!

Now Andrew felt wide awake. He remembered where he left off in the story. Jason, the hero of *Running with Werewolves*, was about to join a werewolf pack.

Andrew had read all but the last few pages. He'd die if he didn't find out what happened. He glanced at his clock. He could skip brushing his teeth for once. And washing his face.

Andrew sat on his bed. His eyes skimmed the words. Jason was in big trouble. He was a werewolf now. But the head werewolf didn't want him in the pack. Jason and the head werewolf were about to engage in mortal combat! Only a werewolf can kill another werewolf. So one of them had to kill the other. Jason didn't stand much of a chance.

Andrew's heart pounded as the snarling head werewolf reached out his huge hairy paws. Reached out and grabbed Jason's neck. He squeezed, tighter and tighter. Choking Jason.

Andrew lifted his eyes from the book to catch his breath—and a hand from behind clutched his neck!

Andrew tried to scream. But no sound came out.

A voice came from behind Andrew. "Be ready in ten minutes!"

It was Emily's voice.

Emily let go of Andrew's neck. Then she reached around and snatched his book.

"Hey!" Andrew cried. He leaped up. But he was too late.

Emily was running out of his room with the book. Andrew chased her. "Give it back!" he cried.

Emily whizzed down the stairs. She stood at the bottom, shaking her head. "Be down here in ten minutes, Andrew," she said. "Or this book is history!"

Andrew sighed. He knew when he was beaten. He plodded back to his room. There, he pulled on a polo shirt and a pair of jeans. Maybe Mrs. Parma had a copy of *Running with Werewolves* in the school library. But probably not. Andrew would have to wait to find out what happened to Jason. He'd have to ask Emily for his book back. She might make him get down on his knees and beg!

Andrew got dressed. All but his sneakers. He felt around under his bed. He thought his sneakers were under there.

His fingers hit something. Something cold as ice. Not a sneaker. Definitely not. Andrew grasped the cold thing. He dragged it out from under his bed—and found himself gazing at a book.

An old black book. It looked important somehow. Boy, did it ever feel cold. So cold it stung his fingers.

The book had no title. Andrew ran his hand over the smooth black leather. *Why does this book feel like a frozen TV dinner?* he wondered. *And how did it get under my bed?*

He opened the book. A blank page stared back at him. Andrew flipped page after page. Blank, blank, blank.

"Andrew?" Mrs. Griffin called from the bottom of the stairs. "What's keeping you, honey? Emily's waiting!"

"Coming!" Andrew called back.

He tossed the book down on his bed. He rummaged around, found his sneakers, and stuffed his feet into them. Maybe he'd take the black book to school with him. Show it to T.J.

But wait. That's who must have put the book under his bed—T.J.! It had to be T.J. It was definitely a T.J. kind of joke.

Andrew slipped his homework papers into his binder. He shoved his binder into his backpack. He reached for the black book. Then he stopped.

He squinted down at the cover.

It had been blank before. Totally blank. He was sure of it. But now spidery letters were beginning to appear. Old-fashioned letters—writing themselves onto the book!

Andrew could only stare and wait as the writing continued.

And then it stopped.

The title was complete.

Andrew felt his blood run cold as he whispered the words on the front of the book:

HOW TO BE A VAMPIRE

GOT FEAR?

MAKE SURE TO PICK UP ALL THE SPOOKTACULAR TITLES IN R.L. STINE'S GHOSTS OF FEAR STREET.